IS IT STILL MURDER
EVEN IF SHE WAS A BITCH?

A DONNA LEIGH MYSTERY BY ROBIN LEEMANN DONOVAN

Published by Gracie Dancer LLC

www.rldonovan.com

Printed in the United States of America

Cover Design by Bozell

Cover Photography Copyright © by MinorWhite Studios

ISBN (eBook Edition): 978 1 943976 03 4
ISBN (Print Edition): 978 1 943976 02 7

Second Edition

DEDICATIONS

To my beautiful bulldog, Gracie, we miss you, sweetheart!
To my dear friends Natalie Corbo and Bonnie Woods,
who taught me the true meaning of courage.

ACKNOWLEDGEMENTS

To my husband, Joe and my Mom, Gloria Knak for working so hard to advise, inspire and support me. To my sister, Trish D'Arcy whose laughter gave me confidence. To my bulldogs, Jazzy and Roxi, who were always there to help keep me going with their unconditional love. And to all the wonderful folks at Bozell, who helped and supported me in this effort as they do every day of my life.

IN MEMORY

Of my Dad, Emil Leemann, who taught me that life should be fun.

TABLE OF CONTENTS

TABLE OF CONTENTS CONT'D

I DIDN'T KILL HER,
BUT THAT MAY HAVE BEEN SHORT SIGHTED

[]

[CHAPTER 1]

Claire Dockens was dead. Wow, that was a shock. When Kyle told me I almost dropped right on the spot. How often is it that someone you've known for years, worked with in the trenches, whose house you've been to several times, drops dead? She wasn't even that old – like early fifties.

If that weren't enough of a bombshell, Kyle's next revelation definitely put me over the edge – "And they say she was murdered." At that point I think I did lose consciousness for a second or two – not enough to make me actually hit the floor – but I'm sure, moments later, I wasn't facing in exactly the same direction as I had been before my momentary lapse.

The next thought that entered my shock-addled head was, "I wonder if they'll suspect me? I mean, it's not like I could stand her."

Then, Kyle said, "Gosh, I hope they won't think I did it."

Kyle Thoroughgood was my colleague and friend at Marcel, the oldest and most revered advertising and marketing consulting firm in Omaha, Nebraska. We'd both been colleagues of the victim a few years prior, and the day that Claire tendered her resignation had been an occasion of mutual celebration. Her mere existence had elicited an intense aggravation in both Kyle and me. She'd openly sought to condemn and abuse us for her own personal sport. With Claire as a colleague, we definitely hadn't needed any enemies. Truthfully, Kyle and I were but two of her multitude of victims since verbally abusive banter was her preferred pastime, but with the two of us she'd taken it to a level beyond. She had elevated her abuse to an art form.

That's when we both heaved a sigh of relief. Hell, the list of suspects would be monumentally huge! Sure we'd be on it – but undoubtedly we'd get lost in the shuffle of characters with sufficient motive.

"So how'd they do it?" I tentatively pressed.

"Bludgeoned as she was leaving a charity dinner," Kyle offered.

"Oh god, that really could have been any of us," I shuddered. "With what?"

Still nodding Kyle responded, "Hasn't been released yet. I don't think they're sure. From what I know they haven't found the weapon and the autopsy is scheduled for tomorrow morning."

"Oh yeah, how'd you find out?"

"Facebook."

That's when my partner Liv walked by with her third coffee of the morning. "Gotta run – late for a meeting," she tossed out, and then, "Shit, does coffee come out of silk?" As she frantically swiped at the growing brown stain on her new couture blouse.

"Hey," Kyle pursued "hear about Claire?"

"I read it on Facebook at 2 a.m. last night when I was finishing

10

the proposal for this meeting. Her poor family!"

Leave it to Liv to give the kind, humanitarian response. Liv Danielsen was my partner and fellow owner of Marcel. I'm Donna Leigh. Ten years prior Liv and I had the amazing opportunity to purchase Marcel, the legendary ad agency that had once grown to global status and revenue before being purchased by a somewhat short-sighted holding company and allowed to idle long enough for Liv, two other partners and myself to buy the company. Over the years, our other two partners had eased out and/or retired. Liv and I hand-picked a third partner who had worked with us to reposition the business and shed the "ad agency" persona that was killing every agency unable to make the jump into the future and the world of social media and one-on-one dialogs with customers: Donny Miller.

"Kyle and I are on a mission to identify the murder weapon."

Liv just rolled her eyes and grabbed a damp cloth. She dabbed at her spreading stain while running toward the already packed conference room.

I turned back to Kyle in time to see Donny motoring up the hallway. "I suppose you know about Claire too?"

One thing about Donny; he was connected. If you needed anything you could count on him to hook you up with the best in the city. With his pervasive human network in place it was virtually impossible to be the bearer of any kind of news to Donny, because there was nothing he hadn't already heard.

"Hell yes, two of my high school buddies were cops on the scene. One of them texted me even before the coroner pronounced her dead. I would have run down to check it out – but he didn't think his CO would be too thrilled. I tried you on your cell. Man, this will really be a blow to the Omaha business community. She was unquestionably one of the smart ones, one of the few I could really respect."

"You're kidding."

"Yeah, she didn't know anything." He smiled impishly. "She sure thought she did though. One thing's for sure – they won't have a shortage of suspects. Hey Donna, now that I think of it, you're probably on the list – you too, Kyle."

Now Kyle and I did the eye roll. Typical Donny. But this time he'd kind of struck a nerve. I could tell by the look on Kyle's face that we were thinking the same thing – would we be getting a visit from a detective anytime soon? Exciting as that may have sounded, we didn't want any public notoriety that would give our clients reason to believe that we could not give them our full focus.

That was when it struck Kyle. He excused himself to call the clients and give them a heads up that the murder victim was one of our former employees. Poor guy, he'd be stuck ducking tough questions while short on information, and forced to appear respectfully sad and inordinately complimentary to a person who made his life hell every chance she got. But that's the way it goes – once a team member always a team member, and even though Claire hadn't been a member of the Marcel team at the time of her death – he wasn't about to speak ill of the dead. Actually, Kyle never speaks ill of anyone. Fortunately for me I can sometimes make him laugh with my blunt and irreverent characterizations of some of our well-deserving colleagues and associates. I'm not as nice as Kyle.

I rolled my eyes at Donny and headed back toward my office passing two puzzled-looking copywriters. One thing was for certain, it would be a while before we lacked a topic of conversation.

[CHAPTER 2]

Later that day I saw Kyle again. He was exhausted from the multitude of discussions on the "topic du jour."

"I can honestly say that nothing got done today," lamented Kyle. "Every second of every meeting and every phone call was completely monopolized by speculation and theorizing over Claire's murder. Naturally, I expected the topic to be addressed, but I'm kind of shocked at the intensity with which it's being dissected over and over. Most of these people never even knew Claire, but they're all hungry for a little intrigue in their otherwise mundane lives. Personally, I'm ready to move on. I mean, I can understand the interest of our staff. Some of them had known Claire for years. Our newest client, Andrea, actually worked here a few years ago and she worked directly with Claire."

"Yes, and as I recall, Claire was the main reason for her leaving. Another suspect!" I volunteered. "How many does that make now? Actually, Kyle, my day has been a bit challenging as well. Not only did I receive phone calls from long lost mutual friends looking for the scoop, I also heard from complete strangers who plucked my name off of the Internet along with a reporter or two. But the highlight of my whole day was the jerk who called to say he was from Coke. He said they had seen our website and some of our client work and we were just the type of agency they wanted for a new product they were planning to launch. He said he wanted to set up a meeting within the next couple of days. Next thing I know, he starts talking about all of the excitement 'down our way.' Smelling a rat, I began to ask a few pointed questions. That clown wasn't from Coke – he was just digging for dirt on the murder. That's about as low as it goes. Hmmph, thought he could pass himself off as a Coke guy - doesn't he know I read *Ad Age?*"

"Oh god, Donna. I'm really sorry to hear that. I guess your day was actually worse than mine."

"Well, either way, I'm starting to think this isn't going to end anytime soon. I think we need a game plan, Kyle."

"What have you got in mind?"

"I've got nothing, how about you?"

"I say we check out the progress on the case, maybe scope out Omaha.com, and see what's kicking around on Facebook. Once we have an idea of where things stand we'll be able to figure out what we should be doing. Let's touch base on our way out, but it should probably be no surprise if it all has to be scratched for a whole new direction in the morning."

"No kidding. And while you're getting up to speed I'll ask Sutter in PR to begin preparing some talking points for all the managers – those reporters are relentless! That should take some time – you know good old Tim, 'Well, we'll have to mention that she graduated from high school with honors.' Sometimes a detail orientation is a curse!"

"You got that right – so should we meet back here in about an hour?"

"Yeah."

[CHAPTER 3]

An hour later we were not much wiser. Kyle had concluded from all his checking that the murder weapon was truly a mystery. Speculation was mounting and the police were hoping that the autopsy would provide some much needed answers.

"So," Kyle started. "What do you think?"

Never one to soft-pedal a dramatic opportunity, I launched into my brilliant plan. "Y'know, Kyle, this won't be the slam dunk that you'd expect. Don't expect to see a murderer holding the smoking gun like in the movies."

"I have to agree with you there – the police certainly have their work cut out for them."

"Well, I was talking to DL – I was on the board of the QCP with her – and she jokingly said, 'Don't you agency folks claim to solve challenging problems? Why don't you take a crack at this murder? Hell, you even knew the victim intimately.' ' Well,' I responded, 'please don't use the term intimately when describing my relationship with the victim – ugh – but we solve business problems

– not police detective, bloody-corpse, physical-evidence, serious-danger, could-get-yourself-killed problems.'

'Well, whatever, but I think you guys should put your money where your mouth is. You do say any problem, so, what about it?'

"I have to admit that the more I think about it - the more I think DL's got something. I mean we know so much about the victim and so many of the people who potentially have a motive. Not only would we be helping ourselves and numerous other potential suspects, but if we solved a murder we'd sure have one hell of a problem-solving case study to show potential clients. Don't you think?"

I could see from Kyle's furrowed brow that I'd gone too far, but he's so nice he can't help giving every idea his full consideration. I knew I'd have at least another five minutes before he began to politely suggest that the events of the day were clearly getting to me and that I needed to go home and get a good night's sleep.

So I pressed on. "I know that right now you're thinking – that is so cold - and you're right. A woman is dead. A horrible, abusive and maniacal woman – but a woman nonetheless. Maybe I got carried away with the case history. Maybe we just need to do this for the sake of all those many poor potential suspects who will be agonizing over the outcome until the real culprit is brought to justice. Or given a ticker tape parade… sorry, sorry."

As usual Kyle's wisdom prevailed, "No, Donna, I can definitely see the logic of giving the police a bit of a hand in this. I'd be a hypocrite if I pretended that she deserved more compassion – although a case history might be a little over the top – but I do have a few reservations. First, Liv and Donny are two of our best problem solvers, we'd normally want them involved in something as huge as this. But I think I can say with complete certainty that if we outline our plan for them they will have us both committed."

"Yes, I see your point. And I do always like to get their insights on these tricky problems. But you're definitely on board – right?"

"Well, yes, I think we should do our best to help get to the bottom of this."

"Okay – then you leave Liv and Donny to me, but first we'd better get ourselves organized. Are you open for lunch tomorrow? By then the press will have some preliminary info from the autopsy and there might be some clue as to the murder weapon. "

"Sure, I have to move one thing and I can do a late lunch tomorrow."

[CHAPTER 4]

"Maybe we should start by making a list of everyone we know without a motive to kill her. Granted there are few – but that might lead us somewhere."

"Sure Donna, you mean like Gil Feund and Clyde Barnhooven, the equally greedy but somewhat dimwitted cohorts in her ill-conceived attempt to take over the agency? They were two people who actually seemed to worship her."

"Funny you should place them on the non-suspect list, Kyle. I'm not convinced that the somewhat hasty exit of Gil and Clyde from Marcel's hallowed halls did not somehow tie back to our victim. I don't think I'd be so quick to put them on the non-suspect list. Actually, now that I think of it, there are some questions that come to mind…"

Gil, Clyde and Claire had been intent on changing the agency to reflect a business model that mirrored past successes. Their vision never came to fruition, because few believe that the past can or should be recreated, and because the trio never had the business acumen and vision necessary to lead anything. Evidence indicated that Claire had ultimately sold the other two down the river in order to advance her own cause. It was not widely known – but the fact remained – Gil and Clyde had been humiliated by the duplicitous Ms. Dockens. Those two were not known for taking things lying down. Frankly, those two were at the top of my list of suspects, but I hated to drag Kyle into the sordid world of agency intrigue and betrayal. Oh well, everyone loses their innocence at some point.

I just couldn't bring myself to burst Kyle's good-hearted bubble.

"You're probably right, Kyle. They did love her. We'll put them on the no-motive list – for now."

"Okay Donna, who else?"

"Ummmm, her husband? The afternoon drive time political talk show DJ?"

"Ooohhh Donna. You know I'm not one to spread dirt, but I just heard some juicy tidbits indicating there might have been trouble in paradise, if you know what I mean."

Wow, this was one unpopular chick. I guess it wasn't just me. Her colleagues hated her, her friends hated her, and apparently her family hated her. We were far from narrowing down the list of suspects. Maybe it was time to take another tack.

"Okay look, Kyle, we're not getting anywhere so let's not waste any more time. Let's plan on meeting at five today and maybe some of those autopsy reports will have been filed and maybe we'll think of something else that's relevant. I'm really starting to feel useless. You know I hate that!"

"Sure Donna, this is pretty discouraging. And let's face it – we only know of Claire's activities up to a point. Since she left the agency to work for that billboard company we really don't know all of the turns that her life has taken. To tell the truth, we've both avoided anything connected to her as much as possible."

[CHAPTER 5]

"Oh God, Donna, I heard from Clovis," groaned Kyle.

"I can only imagine what is going on in that adorable little waifish head."

Clovis was a fascinating character study. Clovis Cordoba Seville was a former Marcel employee. During her tenure at Marcel she made it a point to position herself as a direct rival to Claire. She hailed from a family of Romanian Gypsies and could talk her way out of doing any work at any time. No kidding. It's a formidable skill. I have personally asked her to handle certain clients or new business issues and have been expertly double-talked right out of my request through a brilliant path of circular logic that shakes me to my very core. During Clovis' tenure with the company the rest of us found ourselves busier than we could ever imagine – we never once delegated successfully to her. That gypsy magic comes into play on each of these reversed requests when the inevitable moment of irony comes and Clovis begins to complain that we're shutting her out of these critical career opportunities. Do you doubt that your head can spin around 360 degrees? You need to meet Clovis. I bow to the master!

"Donna she's starting. "

"Oh god, Kyle, what?"

"Clovis is convinced that she's the prime suspect. And let's face it, in her world she's the prime everything. She wants me to help her find the murderer because she's convinced the police are tailing her and bugging her phones and computers. Donna, I can't do this. It was bad enough when she was here, but I cannot have her bugging me day and night because she's convinced that she is the only suspect. Really, I'll start to envy the victim – soon!"

"I hear that, Kyle. Maybe if we can get some answers we'll stumble onto a real lead and you will be spared the torture of Queen Narcissus."

"Don't just say that to keep me from jumping out of this window!"

"Okay then we'd better get to work. What's the word on the autopsy? I checked Omaha.com but nothing had been posted yet. "

"Oh, Okay. I have a friend in the coroner's office. The results of the autopsy were inconclusive. They really don't know what the murder weapon was, but they know the shape of the wound is definitely unusual, and the weapon must be missing, or they'd know, right?"

"Good point. So what have we got? A missing murder weapon and an odd-shaped wound. That's something. Too bad the murder weapon's missing. I'm sure finding it would go a long way toward clearing us. So either the murderer was smart enough to take it when he or she made their escape, or someone picked it up before the police turned up on the scene. Based on the fact that Claire was murdered outside of the Holiday Inn Convention Center on the night of the big annual Boy Scout dinner, her murderer could certainly have been another attendee of the Boy Scout dinner. In fact, who else would have been in that area besides someone attending the dinner?"

"Someone who'd been following the victim," Kyle brooded.

"Great, so basically we've learned nothing."

"Right."

"Maybe we need to start calling on some of the local reporters. They want to talk to us anyway – to get a line on her tenure at Marcel. We just have to be smarter than they are - get more than we give. I'm dying to get more details as to why they're saying her wound was "odd shaped." Hey, maybe Donny and his high school pals can help. Okay Kyle, so you go ahead and call the reporters you know – and I'll start with Donny and his high school posse – sound good? And maybe checking out the crime scene would give us some insights. "

"I guess. That all makes sense, but I'm turning off my cell phone when I go home!"

[CHAPTER 6]

I steeled myself for an early start this morning. Getting Donny and his posse engaged was critical. I waved to Marissa and Shelley. They were sure getting an early start. Need to finish up a few things from yesterday. There's a message. Oh no, it's Clovis.

"Donna, why are they doing this to me? I don't deserve this. Call me immediately!"

Not likely. Rrrrriinngggg.

"Donna Leigh"

"Donna, thank god I got you, it's Clovis." That voice. It went right through me! From across a room Clovis was pretty hot, I had to admit. But once you got in closer there were some undeniable flaws that took a massive toll on the overall experience. The voice for one. It was shrill and sing-songy at the same time. I'm not sure how she did that. And then there was, well her. I'm all for thin. In fact, I spend half of my life working to get or stay thin. But Clovis took thin to an unnatural extreme. Normally clothing looks best on a very thin frame but Clovis is living proof that too thin is not good.

26

Up close, her clothing hung on her like limp laundry swaying in the breeze. If you got a look at her legs you began to fear that a slightly more aggressive step on her part would snap one of those bony twigs right in two. Her hair was a blond lump of frizz with black roots that showed through the thin mass of "stylish" curls. That, however, did not stop Clovis from thinking that her biggest problem in life was the fact that EVERYONE was madly in love with her and plotting how to get her – yes, we're talking men AND women. Her ego did not discriminate.

"Oh hi, Clovis." Why did I come in early? "What can I do for you?"

"Well I suppose you've heard that the police are convinced that I killed Claire!"

"Uh, no. How would I hear that?"

"Everyone's talking about it. Why, Kyle is obsessed with it."

"Really, I didn't get that impression. But, what makes you say that, Clovis? Did they question you for hours? Did they detain you?"

"Uh, no. They haven't contacted me, yet. But you know how intuitive I am, Donna. I just can't help but feel that this whole thing revolves around me. I know they're watching me. Does that surprise you?"

"Actually no Clovis, it doesn't. "

"Donna, I need you and Kyle to help me solve this case once and for all. Let's find the killer and I'll be free once again!"

"Clovis, you are free."

"Oh, but my soul is bound and…"

"Yeah, I get the picture. Sure, Kyle and I will do some checking. Just get some rest Clovis – you've been through a lot."

"Oh, you do understand me, Donna. So few do. Yes, I think your advice is sound. You will keep me apprised of any progress that you make since I am the center of this whole investigation."

"Sure Clovis – we won't make a move without informing you. Just let us do our thing and this will all work out for the best." Of course my best would have included Clovis hanging from the highest yardarm for murdering Claire. There's definitely something to be said for killing two birds with one stone. But Kyle would say that's uncharitable of me. Whatever.

I hung up the phone and shook my head. Then I shook it again. No good – I just couldn't shake Clovis out of my brain. Best to distract myself. Time to see Donny.

When I entered Donny's office he was on the phone with a client "No I don't think you need another TV spot. You've only been running this new campaign for six weeks." Donny motioned for me to sit. "I'm glad you're getting such a good response – but you're far from burnout at this point on the spots running now . Yes, of course we can meet to discuss it. I'll set up a time on Outlook. Talk to you later." Donny looked at me with a grin. "Sometimes they just beg you to take their money. "

"I know, but that's why they trust you so much. They're always so surprised when you talk them out of spending money. "

"Well, far be it from me to talk them out of spending money , but I'd rather they take their extra booty and spend it on expanding their social media program. That's where they've been the most conservative, and they've been getting such a great initial response it makes sense to commit more heavily now that they're establishing a track record. You know if they don't run a heavy enough schedule they will not realize an acceptable return on their investment. Should that occur, they will likely reach the conclusion that social media doesn't work for their business rather than face the unpleasant fact that they just weren't doing it right, but I'm guessing you're not in here to talk about media burnout. What's up? The cops been in to see you yet?"

"Funny. No I actually wanted to ask for a favor, Donny "

I groaned inwardly at the thought of the price this request would extract. Donny looked pensive.

"Relax," I continued, "this is probably something you were planning on doing anyway. I was wondering if you'd mind contacting a few of your high school buddies. The ones most likely to know anything in connection with the murder. "

"You mean my cop friends?"

"Yeah, and anyone else who would know someone or something that could shed some light."

Donny was an Omaha resource unto himself. Born to a respected Omaha family, he spent his school years getting to know pretty much everyone. Wanting to experience a broader geographic culture, he left Omaha to attend college and then waltzed through a series of senior executive positions as he moved from one market to another. By the time Donny made it back to home base he had a wealth of diverse experience and a core network that supplied infinite knowledge on virtually anything. Combined with the extensive local connections that kept him plugged in to anything happening in Omaha, his information network was unstoppable, which came in handy on more occasions than I can remember. The fact was that the numerous members of Donny's extensive national network often sought out his expertise on tricky business problems which frequently brought lucrative assignments into the agency.

"Sure, I'll make some calls. But why are you so intent on gathering all these details? "

"Well, you said yourself – either Kyle or I might find ourselves on the suspect list. The more we know the more we'll be able to defend ourselves successfully."

"Yeah, and a little knowledge is a dangerous thing. Count me in – you know I'm always up for a little intrigue. And I'm sure I'll be able to find out more than you or Kyle." Humility wasn't always his greatest asset – but you had to respect his honesty and those of us who knew him best had seen a much more vulnerable Donny on rare candid occasions.

"No doubt. Let me know what you find out."

[CHAPTER 7]

Back at my office I contemplated my next move. The crime scene seemed the next logical place to look. I dialed Kyle's office and got his voicemail. After the beep, I asked if he could sneak away for an early lunch and check out the scene. As I was hanging up the phone Peg, or Mom as we usually called her when she was out of earshot, walked into my office.

"What are you up to?" Peg grumbled.

"Oh nothing. Kyle and I are just a bit curious."

"Yes, and curiosity killed the cat if you recall."

"Yes, but this cat is not planning on getting close enough to anything to get killed," I retorted.

"And I'm sure that wasn't part of Claire's master plan either, but things happen."

"I couldn't argue with that." Luckily, the phone rang and saved me from further admonition. "Oh, hi Kyle, what do you think?" After a moment of listening I knew that Kyle's schedule was too full to allow for more than a few phone calls and a brief update or two.

So I responded "Sure, I'll just head over there myself – I'd rather not wait to check it out."

When I hung up, Peg was standing across from my desk with her arms crossed and a determined look on her face! I knew that look – whatever was coming was not going to be diverted – under any circumstances. "I'll talk to Babs and the two of us will accompany you."

"That's really not necessary…"

But Peg interrupted before I could finish "I will not hear another word about it. Liv would never forgive me if I didn't keep you from hurting yourself! We'll meet you at the elevators at 11:30 – and you're buying lunch!" There it was. But, in all honesty, my bravado with Kyle was starting to seem somewhat foolhardy – I would be a lot braver with my posse at my side!

True to her word Babs and Peg were waiting at the elevators at precisely 11:30.

"Okay," I exclaimed. "Road trip." And we were off.

Once we settled into my car, Babs and Peg were anxious to talk about all the excitement of the past couple of days. So for the next few minutes the car buzzed with the chatter of three fifty-something menopausal, maybe post-menopausal women – all of us colleagues and all acquaintances of the victim. Peg and Babs were attired in their office uniforms of jeans and a sweater, while I wore my standard black pants and a black t-shirt. My regulation-issue black jacket had been cast off due to an early menopausal heat wave that morning. After spending the bulk of my career in the Northeast, my wardrobe pretty much consisted of all black all the time. Even though that religiously adhered-to uniform did not exist out here in America's heartland, I was now at a stage of life where the slenderizing aspects of all black made it seem like the most logical wardrobe guideline to embrace. Besides, it made accessorizing a breeze!

It was always an awesome experience teaming up with Babs and Peg. Not only will they watch my back against all odds, but they are also two of the hardest working and most reliable people I've ever known. That old Midwestern work ethic was undoubtedly coined after observing these two women on a typical day. They are remarkable.

Babs was a Marcel lifer. She'd been our broadcast producer for over thirty years. In that time she has dealt with some of the most self-absorbed and egomaniacal talent in America. She's handled divas demanding gourmet chocolate and sparkling water, from obscure artesian springs in Oregon and served at the perfect temperature, to thespians raging over being driven in a white rather than the more chic black limo. She not only manages to meet all of their ludicrous and ever changing requirements, she does it with a constant smile on her face. The woman is a magician.

Peg on the other hand runs the whole agency. After over a decade at Marcel no one has yet been able to determine her exact job title because we rely on her for literally everything. Peg has written, designed and proofed ads sometimes on the same day that she is organizing a client luncheon for thirty, and she never breaks a sweat.

When I first arrived at Marcel as the newly recruited media director, I marveled at her ability to juggle so many diverse agency issues so adeptly. My evolution into an ownership position has afforded additional insights into this amazing woman. On more times than I can recall a laborious and difficult meeting of the partners has finally resulted in a solution that, we are sometimes hard pressed to admit, had previously been suggested casually, in passing, by Peg. One can only shake one's head.

As we drove our banter continued. There were occasional exclamations of shock and surprise that were still felt by all, mingled with maternal concerns over our former colleague's family. By the time we arrived at the crime scene, the parking lot of the Holiday Inn Conference Center on 72nd Street we'd all reached the same conclusion. Clearly there was someone out there who felt about Claire the same as we did with one major distinction. He or she was decidedly more proactive.

I parked the car and we walked slowly over to the crime scene. It wasn't hard to miss with the requisite crime scene tape and the legendary chalk outline still in evidence. Suddenly it hit me. This was no joking around. Someone we knew had really been murdered and in a place that was very familiar to us. Over the years we'd all attended numerous luncheons and dinners at this very venue, and poor Claire had been attending the Boy Scout dinner. Her teenage son was an Eagle Scout. I was pretty sure that the other two were feeling as stunned as I was – no one said a word – we just looked on with our mouths hanging agape.

We weren't at the scene more than a minute or two when a nondescript sedan pulled up to us and stopped abruptly, causing us to jump several feet to the side to avoid certain annihilation. Not a smart move for a middle-aged woman with a history of back problems. Oh well, what can you do? I suppose it was better than getting flattened!

Before we had a chance to regroup, an attractive young woman in a plain gray suit stepped out of the vehicle. Peg started to recant the probable injuries she had caused to the three of us – when the newcomer interrupted her, "What are you three doing here?"

Peg's righteously indignant reply came out in force "What business is that of yours? And do you know that you nearly killed us?" not wanting to miss an opportunity to get in her rant.

"What business do you have at the crime scene? Were you connected to the victim?"

Just as Peg was about to raise the ferocity of her diatribe our intruder flashed a badge. "Detective Warren. Now, I will ask you again. What are you doing here?"

"Well Ma'am." I stepped in "We were just paying our respects."

"So you did know the victim?"

"Yes." Said Peg "We used to work with her."

That's when Detective Warren stepped over to her unmarked vehicle, opened the door, and leaned in grabbing the radio handset. She began to talk into the radio – and she was talking about us. At this point Peg must have realized that the smarter move would have been to refrain from voluntarily launching us right into the middle of a murder investigation, and she felt that her statement needed some clarification. So, she stepped over to the driver's side of the car and tapped vigorously on the detective's shoulder. Unfortunately, her earnest attempt to gain the detective's ear had another effect altogether. Upon receiving the final and most forceful tap the detective lurched forward knocking the stick shift into neutral. And you guessed it, the car was parked on an incline. So the car began to roll backwards, gaining momentum by the second. Detective Warren, stuck half in and half out was being pushed down the hill along with the car. I'm willing to bet you've never seen three menopausal women move as fast as we did then. Unfortunately, not fast enough. The car, with detective in tow, kept rolling until it hit the guard rail. The impact sent Detective Warren bouncing wildly about the car interior. By the time we made it down the hill the good detective was borderline conscious and the car was hanging over the guardrail. Babs went over to see if we could separate the car from a tree planted just on the other side of the guardrail, and managed to separate the bumper from the car.

[CHAPTER 8]

After we were released from the station house we called the office to explain why Peg missed her 3 p.m. deadline, Babs missed a photo shoot, and I missed a meeting with Donny and Liv.

Back at the office, we stepped off the elevator to be greeted by Donny beaming from ear to ear. "Wrecked an unmarked car over lunch, huh? And I thought I was doing good because I got a buck off my sub at Quizno's." His laughter could be heard all the way down the hall. As I turned to make my indignant retort, I was greeted by the borderline apoplectic face of Liv coming the other way. She flashed a tense smile at Peg and Babs through gritted teeth and directed me to her office with an "if looks could kill" eye motion.

Once in her office Liv lost no time in launching her full assault.

"What the hell are you doing?"

"Look Liv…"

"That was a rhetorical question! Don't speak. What do you mean by endangering staff and involving them in a murder

37

investigation? Are you crazy?"

"I'm sorry. I guess I was just so paranoid that I could end up a suspect that I wasn't thinking."

"Look you're no more likely to end up a suspect than any of us. None of us could stand her. She didn't treat you and Kyle worse than she treated me. It's just that I didn't let her get to me the way you did. Believe me, I could end up as a suspect every bit as easily as you! Hell, our last fight before she resigned was enough to throw suspicion on me"

Liv's tirade was interrupted by a voice from beyond the doorway. "Very interesting."

" Oh no," I thought frantically as Detective Warren strolled in looking essentially the same with the exception of a few strategically placed BandAids over some painful looking bumps and bruises. I was feeling definite pangs of guilt and I selfishly wondered how anxious she would be to hurt us in return. "Guess I got here at the right time. Anyone else looking to confess while I've got my pad out?" I guessed I would find out!

Liv shot me a dirty look. "Oh, Detective, how are you feeling?" I asked with my best brown-nosing, sugary sweet tone. I was starting to make myself a little nauseous.

"I'm feeling like you and I need to talk about your relationship with Claire."

"Are you sure you're up to it detective? I mean you've had a tough day." This time Liv's face was distorted into an "are you out of your freakin' mind" grimace? But she never said a word. I do admire that self control. The detective and I headed into the nearest conference room for a little chat about the "vic." After years of watching murder mysteries, I was finally going to get the chance to test drive my knowledge of cop jargon.

"So, Ms. Leigh, you wanna tell me what's happening?"

"Let me be perfectly honest here, detective." In hindsight diving right in might not have been the smartest tack, but anyone who knows me will attest that I pretty much tell it like it is. Attempting a less familiar strategy under the circumstances would probably just come back to bite me anyway. "I worked with Claire a few years ago and we got along as well as she did with anyone. Then suddenly, for reasons that I can only guess, she decided to actively assassinate my character. I was just worried that if our history came up it would move me to the top of the suspect list, so I figured I'd see if I could sniff out what really happened, and I can't deny that murder mystery is my favorite genre…"

"Okay, now let me level with you. We know all about your relationship with the victim – it was part of the galloping monologue that that nutsy Cordoba crank has been calling and e-mailing every cop on the force about. At this point there's pretty much nothing we don't know about her working relationships – positive or otherwise."

Clovis – how did that not surprise me?

"So now that we've established your relationship with the vic and you've confirmed it – I think we're good on that note."

"I know, I know. Here's where you tell me to keep my nose out of this investigation or I could get myself killed."

"Not exactly. You're right about our not wanting you to actively pursue suspects and leads, but we know you'll be doing a certain amount of chatting with people in the market. Some of them will seek you out, and some you might want to call yourself. I'd like to hear from you if anything crops up that sounds "off" to you. We are aware that people tend to be more guarded when they know they're talking to an officer of the law. So just keep your ears open and, here, take my card just in case."

"Wow, well sure detective – I'd love to help you guys out in any way that I can."

"And one more thing. Keep 'Cirque de Soleil' away from my squad car. Far away!"

My face turned about eight different shades of red – I'm guessing it hit about a Pantone 185 Red. Just to clarify, Pantone numbers are how we in the ad biz identify colors. Every color has a number and that gives us a tight control on the quality of all printed pieces, 185 is slightly brighter than a fire truck. Not my best color!

It took a few seconds for the accompanying heat in my face to dissipate. "Oh absolutely, detective – no problem with that – I couldn't agree more. We're really very sorry."

"Save it. And be careful. You never know."

[CHAPTER 9]

I saw Detective Warren to the elevator and turned around just in time to see Kyle approach. His face was a deep shade of red as he hurried toward me.

"What happened?" he urged.

"What, you didn't hear?"

"I've been in meetings up until a few minutes ago. My phone was ringing as I walked back to my office. I picked up the receiver and was barraged with an unintelligible tirade from Clovis."

"Clovis? What was she ranting about?"

"Something about three clowns who wrecked an unmarked cop car bringing unwanted attention to her. She wants us to try to remember her and behave ourselves with more decorum so we don't cause her any more problems than she already has."

"Amazing. She never ceases to surprise me. It really is always about her isn't it?"

I spent the next few minutes briefing Kyle on our crime scene road trip and the visit from Detective Warren, remembering to warn him that Liv's patience was starting to wear thin. Kyle's next utterance was music to my ears.

"So we've got the green light to keep investigating from Detective Warren?'

"That's how I read it."

Did I mention that ad people are expert at putting the right spin on everything? Satisfied that we were officially cleared to proceed we got down to business. Kyle briefed me on the few phone calls he'd been able to sneak in between meetings.

"I talked to Rod Carlin. He was the Ad Club President the year that Claire served on the board. They keep in touch and he occasionally threw some free lance work her way. Rod had the feeling that something big was going on with Claire and saw that she was starting to get visibly nervous. He had coffee with her last week and she was very distracted and kept losing her thought mid-sentence. Naturally, Rod was concerned, so he tried to probe about her health and family concerns. When he touched on work she practically ripped his head off and got even more paranoid. Rod had also heard that the outdoor company where she worked was having some zoning issues that could have a major financial constraint on their ability to move forward and add to their billboard inventory in key areas. "

"But she wouldn't really be involved in zoning issues would she?"

"Well, maybe they've given her more responsibility than we were led to believe. Or maybe she was allowed to buy in, and she's worried about her nest egg."

"Interesting. But you're right about one thing – we're just guessing here. We need something more solid to go on." I was starting to sound like a real detective – and Kyle didn't even flinch so I must have pulled it off!

Together we made a contact list of people who might have more inside information on the outdoor company. We agreed that I would call some of Claire's colleagues in the sales department and Kyle would try some of the other ad agencies that dealt directly with her. I would also see what people at the competitive outdoor companies had to say. There was definitely a lot to do! As if on cue, that's when Peg walked in.

"I hope I'm not disturbing you. I was waiting for a chance to get your ear and I wanted to find out about Detective Warren's visit." Kyle excused himself to get to the phone and I filled Peg in on what Warren had said. She looked extremely relieved. Then she switched gears.

"You know, something occurred to me while we were at the crime scene, but with everything that happened…"

"Yes. I was there, you don't have to remind me. But what did you notice?"

"Well, it's a little thing, but I noticed that the actual scene was on the opposite side of the building than where Claire always parked. Back when she worked with us and we drove to a charity luncheon together, she picked the absolute most inconvenient door for us to enter. When I complained, she told me to 'stuff it' because she was not about to park her precious car in the congested parking lot where all of the other 'idiots' put theirs."

43

"Yep, that sounds just like her. Are you sure she still felt the same way about her car?"

"Well, of course I can't say for sure, but she did just get another new car last month, so I would imagine…"

"You know, Peg, I think that's an excellent point. I think that's just the type of thing the detective was talking about, but maybe we should keep a list and call her when we have two or three observations to share. What do you think?"

"Oh, I agree. But there is something else. Babs noticed that there was a ton of mud in the chalk outline of the body. Like she had stepped in a pile of mud right before she got killed. "

"Okay, I'm not getting the point here. Are we sure it was mud from her shoes?"

"Oh, we're sure all right. Babs said there was a mud outline of a shoe. It definitely looked like a woman's shoe and it was bigger than a Buick – you remember what gargantuan feet Claire had?" I nodded. Her feet were tremendous, yet she always insisted on finding those delicate little fashion shoes – and they were NOT easy to find in her off-the-chart-size – so she would never even go near a speck of dirt on the carpet to protect her precious fashion statements? I certainly did remember that!

"And there's more," Peg continued. "Where would she find mud from the convention center to the parking lot – there was none!"

"Peg, you two amaze me! Excellent observations! I think now we do need to call Detective Warren. Should we all call her together?"

"No, you go ahead. I think Babs and I have had enough of the good detective for one day."

"Well, okay, but great work you guys!"

I called Detective Warren to fill her in on Peg's and Bab's observations. She seemed genuinely appreciative.

"Yeah, we knew about the mud – but not her obsession with protecting her precious shoes – that does give the whole mud issue cause for more attention than we'd previously thought. Thanks for calling. We'll let you know if we have any further questions on the mud and the shoes. And you're right – she did have delicate little fashion shoes in a size big enough for Shaquille O'Neal. If we hadn't all seen Claire's feet ourselves we would likely have assumed that her murderer was a transvestite hooker!"

[CHAPTER 10]

Back in my office I started thinking about what we now knew. We knew that Claire parked in a place she normally wouldn't and that she had mud on her shoes that would not have been there in the normal course of attending that charity dinner. We also knew that the murder weapon was missing and the mark made by the weapon was unusual and difficult to identify. Finally, we knew that something related to business had caused an inordinate amount of tension for Claire in the weeks leading up to her death. I was pretty impressed by how many facts we'd uncovered.

It felt good to have so much information that could help Warren, but it was really frustrating that we were still missing so much that none of the puzzle pieces could, as yet, be connected. We needed to know more. It was time to get on the horn with some of those outdoor sales reps, so for the next two hours that's exactly what I did.

I talked to Claire's colleagues at the outdoor company, Toto, the competitive reps and some of the reps who took a more active role in the ad club – since that was such a big focus for Claire. It was an exhausting two hours, but not entirely unfruitful. The hardest part was taking the company line and treating the victim with the reverence that I genuinely reserve for my teammates. We would never trash a colleague or a former colleague. So as far as they knew, Claire was my best bud. Wow, I would have to wash my mouth out with soap when I got home. But, I think I learned some key pieces of intelligence, so I guess it was worth all the white lies. In this case, white lies hardly seemed an adequate description – maybe more like off-white and gleaming like the teeth in a giant Cheshire cat smile. Let's face it, I had taken lying up several notches in order to convince anyone that I genuinely cared about Claire. But, back on point, I had definitely learned that Claire was having some major business tension. In fact she and her much heralded position at Toto would very likely have parted ways within weeks according to two of her more loquacious colleagues, and, big surprise, they couldn't stand her either. Oh, they didn't actually come out and say anything derogatory. But, when you've known Claire for as long as I have, you recognize the signals.

"So you were originally going to drive to the charity event with her?" I quizzed.

"Yeah, the boss was gonna make..I mean I said I wouldn't mind..," stumbled Molly. I got the picture. It was company line day and we were all taking it! You have to respect that.

I didn't think I would get much more out of these reps. Maybe Donny's contacts would be able to shed some light. As I entered Donny's office he was just finishing a spreadsheet with next year's budget. Two of our more junior IT guys wasted no time in beating a hasty retreat out of Donny's infamous den. They were just happy to have escaped alive!

"We'll have some capital expenses next year, so I want to review all the projections at least one more time before finalizing, I will try to allocate capital expenses so they're staggered by quarter," Donny ruminated.

"Sounds good, if that creative printer can just hold out until mid-year," I countered.

"So I'm guessing you're here for my update on 'As the Dead Shrew Turns'?" He asked, very proud of himself. I nodded. "Well, you're in luck! My police buddy from the scene gave me some info on the QT." I smiled. If nothing else, Donny was having the time of his life.

"Okay, what'd he say?" I urged, playing into Donny's overdeveloped sense of theater.

"She had a huge fight with her new boss and he was about to can her. She was in a panic because she knew that her prospects for a sizable salary were negligible in this market."

"Yeah, not for lack of good jobs," I interjected.

"No," agreed Donny. "Even she was starting to realize that she'd burned more than her share of bridges – to the ground – and scattered the smoldering ashes…"

"I hear that. She never believed in assassinating anyone halfway," I encouraged. "But was she really aware that it was starting to catch up with her?"

"According to my buddy. Apparently she'd seen the writing on the wall and had started a job search. I guess some people were pretty blunt about why they wouldn't even consider her. One guy even told her that he knew she was fairly capable, but that he was in no position to replace the other 70 staff members that would leave if he brought her on board," he stated with a smirk.

"Holy crap, are you serious?"

"Swear to God those were his exact words."

"Holy crap!"

That's all I could get out. Judging from the look on Donny's face, he was as shocked as I. We mumbled something unintelligible and I stumbled my way out of his office. The shock clearly written on my face.

On the way out I bumped into Liv.

"Hey, have you got a sec? I heard something that I think will interest you," Liv offered eagerly.

"Uh," I grunted (it was the best I could do) as I followed Liv into her office.

Liv shot me a curious look and then went valiantly on to relay her big news. She had been attending one of the many community board meetings that occupy so much of her already guarded time when she picked up a tidbit that related to the murder. As a partner, Liv gave 350%. She worked like a dog both day and night. No one in the company had escaped Liv's infamous 3 a.m. e-mails.

Today, Liv had on one of her many colorful, cool, and trendy fashion ensembles. As "black on black," as I'd come to be known, Liv was similarly known for her explosion of color. She wore her colors proudly and carried them off as comfortably as other people wore their skin. For the first time that day I noticed a new getup that was sure to make fashion history. A pale pink pencil skirt with coordinating blouse topped by a jacket of concentric ovals of varying sizes, sporting a bronzy brown hue, a stark white and a hint of the pink in the skirt. Her feet were adorned with a pair of killer pink pumps in a shade dark enough to offer a sizable contrast without a scintilla of clash. Her pink circular earrings, in the same shade as the pumps, were the size of large golf balls which also varied in circumference to compliment the circles hanging from her multiple chain necklace. Man, she had flair! I could never figure out when she had time to shop. Liv was just entering the peri-menopausal set and she was not about to give in without a fight!

"She was getting a divorce," Liv announced piously. "You know how I hate gossip but this really shocked me."

"What?" I whimpered dazedly. I was just starting to shake off my shock from Donny's bombshell. Maybe I wasn't as tough as I thought.

"Claire," Liv reiterated. "I heard she was in the process of getting a divorce."

"WHAT!!!" I bellowed.

"I said…," Liv started again.

"Never mind. I heard you the first two times. But I… I can't believe it," I stammered.

"Came from an unimpeachable source," Liv countered.

"Knowing you I don't doubt that for a second. I'm just – what my grandmother used to describe as dumbfounded."

"I know – right?"

"Wow, how far along were things? Who wanted it? Had anyone

moved out yet?" I was getting my momentum back.

"Not sure. I don't think things had deteriorated far enough for them to be at the 'move-out' stage yet. They were all about keeping the kid in the dark at all costs. Trying to keep him wrapped in a protective bubble. But you know that whole Protestant – wait for the last minute to tell the kid what's going on – mindset? When he probably knew before either of them did. You know the carefully crafted plan that inevitably blows up in the parents' face?" she offered.

"Oh yeah – how to do it right – the wrong way."

Just as she was about to respond, Liv's phone gave a familiar ping. "I just got a text from my source. It says he was dumping her and she was livid. Ouch. With her pride that had to smart."

"Well Liv," I started tentatively, "Kyle and I have kind of been working quietly to help the police come up with some leads."

"You think I don't know that? After all these years I know you too well to think you'd ever leave this one alone."

"And you're okay with it?"

"Don't really see much choice," she ventured. "But honestly you know I would do whatever I could to help."

"Really, you're in? 'Cause we could really use your help."

"It's not like you're going to leave me out of something this big," she declared smugly. "And besides, thanks to you, the other two Pointer Sisters, and your afternoon escapade, I've made the suspect list myself. Remember?"

"Now that you mention it… I'm really glad you're working with us, Liv. If nothing else, it should be a challenging problem to solve."

Is It Still Murder, Even If She Was a Bitch?

"All right, give me what you've got," she smiled. You could never keep Liv too far away from a challenge!

[CHAPTER 11]

Back in my office, I reflected on the day's progress with some satisfaction. We'd found some significant information. Plus, we had the whole team on board. Just as I was about to reach around and pat myself on the back for my masterful team-building skills, the phone rang.

"Donna Leigh," I purred still feeling very self satisfied.

"Hi Donna, it's Peg. "

"Where are you Peg?"

"Babs and I are at the funeral and I think there's something you should know," Peg whispered.

"Please tell me it doesn't involve any police cars or guard rails," I implored as the color began rapidly draining from my face.

"Oh, no, nothing like that," Peg assured me. I could feel my facial color begin to stabilize when Peg added, "Well, Babs did bump into one of the pallbearers in our haste to exit the church." Shit, color back to draining. "He'll have a nasty bruise but no harm done otherwise."

"You're sure?" I ventured tentatively.

"Positive. That's not why I'm calling. I thought you should know that the victim's self-involved jerk of a husband, Garth, was flashing intimate looks all through the service with someone we all know, and poor, big-footed Claire not even in the ground yet. And man, talk about big feet! They had to get a casket with a conspicuous bump out in order to fit those canoes in at all. It's supposed to be a design feature but anyone who knew her..."

"PEG! Who, who, tell me who!" I barked.

"Oh yeah right. It was Clovis."

"Are you freakin' kidding me?" I shouted. "You can't be serious! " Now I was bellowing. "Oh never mind. That woman will never cease to amaze me. Why won't I learn?"

"Tell me about it. I wanted to text you right in the middle of the service, but my phone makes this little ding sound, so I thought it would be tacky," Peg lamented.

"Good call. Well this is certainly an interesting turn of events. Do you think anyone else noticed?"

"Funny you should mention that. Clovis brought another woman to the service. I'd say she was a friend but I didn't think she had any. It wasn't anyone that I recognized from this market. I think she just brought her as a beard so that no one would take undue notice of Clovis herself. Anyway, this woman must have fractured her elbow with all of the times she jabbed Clovis. I think it was at least one jab per look.

"Now THAT'S interesting! I wonder who the woman was."

"Well, Babs and I are heading back to the church. There will be a light tea served in the basement. We're going to pay our respects to her dirtbag husband and see what else we can find out. The identity of Clovis's friend will be high on our list. I'll see you before the end of the day." And with that, Peg was off.

I knew Kyle would be blown away by this news. I thought if I hurried I could catch him between meetings. Sure enough, he was just finishing a phone call as I plunked myself down in his visitor's chair. Kyle had one of the more enviable offices in the building. It wasn't that it was much nicer than any of ours but it was decorated by Kyle – and that made it better. The rest of us gave it our best shot and we all had pretty cool spaces that aptly reflected our quirky personalities and our yearning to push design boundaries, but Kyle's office looked as though it had been decorated by an acclaimed professional. A spartan amount of sleek modern furniture arranged in a functional, artistic, but extremely comfortable grouping with a splash of original artwork to add a touch of color to the otherwise bleak walls. You had to envy his gift.

His design talents were clearly not limited to office decor. Kyle himself was a fashionista's dream. His sense of masculine style was equal to his office design expertise. Dress or casual, he was always perfectly coifed and attired. His glasses and other accessories were always the most fashionable. And to top off the entire image, although he was but a few short years behind me in age, beneath that fashion know-how he was blessed with the raw material of a GQ model. Guys like that are never super sweet – he was one in a million!

55

"Kyle, you won't believe what Peg and Babs picked up at the funeral service!" I crowed.

"Clovis and the creep. I know. That was my third phone call about their scandalous behavior. Just wait until that lunatic calls me again! I will never sit through another one of her insane, ranting, rambling monologues…"

I can't deny I was feeling a little let down that my big scoop had been scooped by someone else. How could you not? But no time for ruffled feathers. There was too much to discuss. I filled Kyle in on everything I had learned since we last talked, and then he filled me in on his day – the interesting part anyway.

"After my 9 o'clock meeting this morning, I had a message from a former co-worker, Jeremy. He told me that he was now calling on Toto, the outdoor company where Claire had been employed, " Kyle began.

I listened with rapt attention. This murder was turning out to be an interesting little distraction from the day-to-day, business-as-usual world.

"So I called him right back," Kyle went on. "He'd heard that I was helping the cops dig up info on the victim and had a tidbit he was anxious to share." Man this is a small town sometimes! "Naturally I encouraged him to continue. He said that he'd called on Claire's boss, Collin, a few weeks ago. While he was sitting in the waiting room just outside of Collin's office he started to hear some voices but couldn't make out what they were saying. After a few moments the voices grew louder and the invectives flew faster. It became clear that it was an argument between Collin and a woman."

"Bet I can guess what woman."

"Jeremy said," Kyle continued, "near the end, the voices became loud enough for him to hear a few very hostile accusations that Collin was clearly hurling at the woman. Something about impropriety and illegality. He even mentioned jail time. That's when Jeremy took off."

"What?"

"Yeah, he felt stupid sitting there listening, and didn't want to be around when the door opened, so he decided to spend some time in the men's room until he could re-emerge with a clear conscience and a clear escape plan."

"Spineless – but not stupid!"

"Too true. And he said he was embarrassed to say anything to the police, but he'd be okay if I did," finished Kyle.

"So Collin and Claire were having more trouble than we realized," I declared triumphantly.

"Well, that's just it. Jeremy said he never put two and two together and figured that it had to be Claire until a week or so later when he heard the rumor about her probably getting the axe – and by that I mean fired. We still don't have a handle on the murder weapon, and by handle…"

"Yeah, I get it. So it's not even definite that it was her?" I grunted, feeling deflated again.

"Well, it pretty much had to be her. But you're right we don't have 100% confirmation, " Kyle admitted.

"Do you think this warrants a call to Warren?" I ventured.

"Maybe we should wait until we have some other leads. I'd hate to call and say, "Now we don't know for sure it was Claire, but..."

"Good point. We'd look pretty amateurish," I agreed.

"Let me hasten to point out that...," Kyle rejoined.

"No need," I assured him. "I know we're amateurs, but the way this is going I think I'll be earning my Official Nancy Drew Membership ring in no time."

"You'll pardon me if I don't hold my breath for my Hardy Boys secret message pen. I guess I'm not feeling as optimistic about all this as you seem to be."

"I'd say it's less optimism and more totally lame motivational ramblings. Not working, huh?"

"Not really. Sorry Donna. Maybe we'll learn more after I have a chance to make all of my phone calls," Kyle offered eagerly. What a sweetie he was, always trying to cheer me up no matter how low he felt.

"Okay, let's regroup at the very end of the day. We'll see what else crops up by then."

[CHAPTER 12]

By the time I got back to my office both Babs and Peg were standing there waiting. They were anxious to fill me in on the rest of the dirt from the funeral. Wow, even in my head I cringed at my own cheap pun.

All dressed up in somber colors, Babs and Peg barely resembled the two lovely and endearing ladies I knew so well, but rather some old maid school teachers from a bygone era. Not to worry – once the conversation started they were right back to being their usual enigmatic and charmingly amusing selves.

Peg started, as usual. "Well, we had some very interesting conversations at that church basement tea, I don't mind telling you!"

"Yeah, it got even more interesting," shared Babs conspiratorially.

"A lot of those people noticed the goo-goo eyes between hubby and Clovis, but they said that's just her. She does that with everyone in any kind of spotlight, not at all discriminating." Nice huh? Five minutes with that one and anybody would need a shower...or undoubtedly a tranquilizer! Peg continued, "But here's something real interesting. Remember how I told you that she brought a friend with her?" I nodded my assent. "Well, some of the folks workin' on hubby's talk show say it was the friend that he was foolin' around with. Apparently she was the one using Clovis as a beard, not the other way around, and that sap would do anything to get herself further into the limelight, so she was happy to jump right in and buddy up to 'the other woman'! That just makes my skin crawl," she finished while briskly rubbing both of her arms up and down.

"No kidding? Well, that was certainly worth waiting for." I was back in high spirits – things were starting to percolate again! "Who is she? And who knew about her? Did Claire know?" I couldn't get the questions out fast enough.

Peg laughingly responded, "Well, it seems she worked with hubby at the station – she's the new local sales manager, and, as far as I can tell, we are the only ones who didn't know."

Peg stopped to take a breath and I jumped in with, "So Claire knew."

"We think so."

"Oh come on, we don't know for sure?" I could feel my spirits starting to dip. Maybe this was a low blood sugar issue, red face, white face, spirits up, spirits low. I made a mental note to get a blood test. Gotta keep checking those hormone replacements. You want to be sure you're getting enough, but too much and you could make the Boston Strangler seem shy and retiring. Hmmmm, that gave me another idea about possible suspects. But that probably didn't help my case any so back to the matter at hand.

"I'm not sayin' we don't know," Peg waffled, "just that we can't say for absolute sure. I mean it's pretty common knowledge that they were getting a divorce, so the odds are good that wifey knew about the pretty new LSM (Local Sales Manager). Don't you think?"

I did. But would Warren? "I'm sure you're right, Peg. It's too much of a coincidence to think that they were divorcing for anything more serious than that."

"More serious," Babs was intrigued "Have you got somethin' more serious than adultery?"

"Well, only IF we can confirm that Claire was the one Collin accused of 'illegalities.' We could be talkin' something more serious," I shared.

"Oh yeah, Collin was at the funeral," Peg anxiously spouted.

"And?" I encouraged.

"And he looked like Charles Manson at Roman Polanski's VIP tent!"

"That would be pretty uncomfortable," I observed.

"Oh no, what he was doing requires a whole new word for uncomfortable. It was like he took a whole bottle of Phillips Milk of Magnesia before he left home, and then had a bowl of Eddie's four alarm chili on the way over. That man could not sit still and could not look another person in the eye. Far as I know he never made it over to the grieving widower and he bolted out of there as though his pants were on fire!"

"Hmmm, " I pondered. It was getting late – that was the best I could do. "Thanks guys, once again you've proven to be the best detectives we've got."

"Well, there's one more thing, right Babs?"

"Yeah Donna, that's not all."

"Do tell – don't keep me hangin'."

With her most serious demeanor Peg proceeded to fill me in on the fact that some unusual work was being done at Claire's house. Her informant had nixed the idea that they were fixing it up to sell for the divorce. It was a pretty new, cookie cutter house that had barely had time for the newly planted bushes to bloom. Good point. Peg went on to suggest that the three of us attempt another road trip to go and look at the victim's house. I agreed that it was something we should see for ourselves but was a tad nervous after our last road trip. None of us had time to cool our heels in the pokey for an afternoon. After extracting promises of being on their best behavior, I agreed to meet Peg and Babs at Claire's house at 8 a.m. the next morning. What could happen?

[CHAPTER 13]

After a quick bathroom break I headed back to my office to regroup for our next update. I got to my office door and froze. There, stuck to my computer monitor was a Post-it note that read "snoops die." I had to sit down as I could feel myself starting to hyperventilate. At that moment, Kyle appeared at my doorway. He could see right away that something was wrong so he rushed in only to skid to a stop as he noticed the sticky note.

"Oh god, Donna. Are you all right?"

"No."

"I, um, what do you think?" Kyle sputtered.

"I'm having a heart attack?"

"Understandable. Anything else?" Kyle pressed.

"The murderer works at Marcel?" I choked.

"Or, JQH downstairs," Kyle offered.

JQH was the parent company, a large global advertising services holding company, from whom we had bought ourselves back a decade earlier. They remained our penny-pinching landlord and unwilling neighbor. When we had all been part of one company the folks downstairs had operated our back office function as they had for Marcel offices all over the world. Now completely separated from our parent, we resided in the same building much as a long divorced couple unable to afford separate dwellings. JQH upper management tolerated us as sublessees for our hefty monthly rent check. Staffers at JQH enjoyed the lively, expressive presence our creativity lent to their otherwise drab and boring office parties. Unfortunately the majority of the newer folks, the ones with whom we'd never worked side by side, saw us as Moriarty to their Holmes. For some reason we were the enemy; to be feared when they were forced to approach us and to cower from us in the dreaded shared elevator. Only a handful of the JQH employees who had formerly known us as colleagues and co-workers were still able to behave with any kind of human demeanor in our presence. And, as in any good zombie movie, we shuddered when in the presence of the JQH undead, the majority of the drones who appeared to have no soul – and certainly nothing that resembled a personality. Creepy.

"Maybe," I croaked, still pretty shaken.

"Well," Kyle continued "At any rate I think we need to notify Detective Warren about this development."

"You know what I'm thinking, Kyle?" I was starting to regain my composure. "I think you and I should drive down to the station to talk to Detective Warren about this. Maybe when we're down there we'll pick up on something more substantial – right now I feel as though we're just tilting at windmills."

"Um, yeah, I suppose we could. We could bring the Post-it with us." Kyle rejoined. "And we'll have to be very careful in transporting it, wouldn't want to mess up any fingerprints."

"True, true," I acknowledged. "But it seems unlikely that if the perp is an employee here, (I shuddered deeply) or at JQH, they would be in the system."

"Listen to you, Miss Marple," Kyle crowed. "The perp might not be in the system." This was so typical of Kyle. He wanted to make sure that I was in good spirits as we prepared to make our way over to the station, and Kyle knew that nothing could raise my spirits more than being compared to my childhood hero, Miss Marple. Now get that vision right out of your head – I don't LOOK anything like her. In fact, even as age is creeping up on me I still look a good 40 years younger than that inspirational dowager. I aspire to think like her, NOT look like her or any other of Agatha Christie's brilliant and stalwart detectives.

Kyle found an unused rubber glove in the front closet and a baggy to transport the note. So with evidence in hand we made our way over to the station and Detective Warren. As luck would have it, she'd just arrived and was ready to hear our news.

"So what's up?" the good detective started. We confidently produced our well-preserved evidence and shared the details surrounding its discovery. I knew that watching all those murder mysteries would pay off one day! Warren asked, "Are you sure it wasn't one of your smart-ass staff members just goofin' around?"

Oh crap. Kyle and I just looked at each other. Why didn't we think of that? Now we felt like idiots. Of course that was the most likely possibility. Aside from Donny there were numerous other jokesters that could easily have pulled a stunt like this. Man did we feel dumb, and for once, we were genuinely speechless.

Seeing the growing embarrassment that Kyle and I were experiencing, Detective Warren offered, "Of course we can't take any chances. We'll dust for fingerprints and keep them on file. If we get far enough to see a courtroom, this piece of evidence could come in very handy."

Despite her best efforts to minimize our humiliation, Kyle and I merely grumbled our responses dejectedly. "No really," offered the detective, "this could be important."

Nice of her, but that was one quick trip back to humble. Here I was thinking that my dogged determination and intuitive detecting had scared the killer into thinking I was getting close. I was a real threat. I was starting to fancy myself the attractive young sleuthing niece that Miss Marple never had. What an idiot! I could sense that Kyle was not faring any better. Talk about a reality check. We had to get our egos under control and stop romanticizing this thing, or we'd be of absolutely no help in identifying Claire's killer.

As Kyle and I were waiting for our faces to return to normal from the brilliant shades of purple and red they had turned, Detective Warren's phone rang. She picked up, "Yeah, I'll be right there. I've gotta run for a minute. You two wait right here."

Wishing to shrink into the floorboards, Kyle and I remained mute as we obediently waited for Warren. We didn't have to wait long. From the next office came the sound of a phone ringing. "Detective Murphy," we heard. "Yeah, yeah that's right. The vic was about to get charged with fraud by the insurance company that covered all the outdoor boards at Toto." Interesting. "Yeah, there was a big fight about it the morning of the murder. We think she was yelling at the insurance company investigator. Yeah, we're checking the phone records right now." Suddenly I was feeling much better. I glanced over at Kyle to see renewed vigor in his pose and a gleam in his eye. We were back!

Detective Warren sensed it the second she walked in. "All right you two – what just happened?" she demanded.

"Why nothing, detective," I innocently responded. "We've just been sitting here waiting for you."

"Do I look like I was born yesterday?" Warren countered, "I haven't been a cop all these years to be fooled by a pair of amateur sleuths like you." That hurt.

"So Claire was being charged with fraud?" Kyle valiantly interjected.

"Oh, I see. You thought as long as you were here you'd pick up a few crumbs by eavesdropping."

"Gee, detective. We were just sitting here…"

"You can't help hearing…"

"All right, all right," she sighed; and then much more sternly, "But you leave that line of questioning to the professionals, that does NOT concern you! Do I make myself perfectly clear?"

"Oh yes. Hey I was scared senseless by a sticky note. You don't think I would purposely go after a dangerous killer, do you?" I quipped.

"Let's just say it wouldn't surprise me all that much," she mused. "You two seem to be having way too much fun with this whole thing."

I had to give her that. Our hubris in finding our "huge clue" had exposed our excitement over the whole puzzle-solving element afforded by Claire's brutal murder. We needed to dial it back a few hundred notches, but first we needed to find out who'd been on the other end of that phone during the fight!

We said our good-byes to Warren. "I'll call you if we turn up any interesting fingerprints from that note," she offered. I couldn't help but feel that was a deliberate shot. I wouldn't be as quick to run down to the station the next time anything unusual came to light. Kyle and I spent the next few minutes devising a game plan to get more information about the fraud charge. We were sure Detective Warren would be grateful for our help on this. Even if she didn't realize it yet. As we prepared to drive away, each to our respective homes, I remarked, "Humiliating, yes, but at least we've picked up our 'something more substantial'!"

[CHAPTER 14]

The next morning at the office, I noticed Donny's not-for-profit team was in the small conference room. As I walked by, their meeting appeared to be just breaking up. "Hey Donna," he yelled. "What was up with the threatening Post-it?"

"That was you, you bastard?"

"Hey slow down, what are you talkin' about?"

"Did you put that note on my monitor to be funny?"

"No way, whatdya mean? I thought it was a threat."

"So did I until Detective Warren pointed out that it could have been some jackass comedian from right here."

"Unh unh, it was real, swear to god."

"Why do you say that Donny?"

"I, uh, well now I don't really know, but give me a minute and I'll figure it out. Oh yeah, now I remember. I walked in to ask you a question and the post-it wasn't there. Then, a minute or two later I walked back to leave a copy of a report that Lynn printed out for us and there it was. I looked around, you know just from instinct, and I kind of jogged out to the lobby. As I rounded the corner to the elevators I saw someone getting on – it didn't look like anyone I'd ever seen before and he had a sort of furtive look about him. I bolted over to get a better look but the elevator doors had closed. So, I sorta just assumed that he'd been up there to leave the note. I asked the first five people I saw – you know the ones who sit nearby – if anyone knew who he was or why he was there. None of them had even noticed him. So.."

"So what did he look like?" I bellowed.

"Wish I'd gotten a better look. Sort of average. He was dressed casually and had a hat on that covered his head and his face, but I didn't really get a good look.."

"Well anyway, we know it's a he. That's something."

"Yeah I'll let you know if anything else comes to me – but I doubt it. He looked like your typical delivery guy, kind of casual, not too noticeable."

"Okay. Well I'm not sure if I'm happy to have been validated or sorry that I'm now scared out of my mind."

I went to find Kyle and fill him in on the new information. He suggested that we call Warren with this sobering piece of news. After 15 minutes on the phone with Warren we were both ready to call it quits and run home. She warned us that we now had to take things very seriously. We were clearly posing a threat to someone involved in the case and it was someone who had access to our office without being noticed. She suggested that we beef up security. What security? I would have to talk to Donny about those personal screamer alarms that he was always ranting about. Before this I'd thought them ridiculous, but I guess Donny was right, and maybe we could talk to JQH about reprogramming the elevator to require a special key card to get onto our floor, like they did with their second floor double secret accounting division. It would be a pain with clients and vendors going in and out, but I didn't see how anyone would feel comfortable after this without it. Maybe we'd have to hold a special staff meeting to instruct everyone on emergency security measures for the duration of this investigation. I'd talk to Liv and Donny and see what they thought.

[CHAPTER 15]

The next morning at eight I arrived at Claire's house, as Peg, Babs and I had planned. There, waiting for me, was Peg's minivan, complete with Peg, Babs and Liv inside. That was a surprise.

"Liv? I wasn't expecting you," I tentatively began.

"You didn't really think I'd let the three of you out on your own after what happened at the crime scene did you?" Before I had a chance to respond she continued, "Besides, I kinda did some detective work when I was in college, and I was pretty capable. Anyway, why should you three get all the excitement? I thought we'd work on this together," she gushed to a close.

"Well, yeah, you know we'd love to have you work with us. But you're always so slammed we just figured you couldn't break free."

Just as I said this, Liv's phone began to ring. Peg and Babs looked at me and rolled their eyes.

"Oh, hi honey. Yes, I left the car keys on the table near the front door. Now you come right home after you buy those jeans, I don't want you just riding around." Liv was clearly talking to her daughter, the high school senior.

There stood the four of us, Babs, Peg and I in our practical, down and dirty work jeans, sweats and hiking boots. And then there was Liv. Oh, she was in jeans all right, designer jeans with a cut on the bias jacket in emerald green with a wide white belt. Her accompanying jewelry was a series of enormous balls in emerald green and white hanging off of her ears, neck and wrists from silver chains. Need I say that the spike heeled, emerald suede boots were the perfect accent to her "right out of the pages of 'W' " ensemble? The outfit was killer!

"Sorry guys. What are we doing?" Liv dove right back into our mission. Before we had a chance to respond we heard a tinkling sound. Liv looked down – she had a text. "Hang on guys, it's Lake. He needs my help to complete an estimate before his 9:30 meeting. Why don't you guys get started, I'll join you in a sec."

Now we were just laughing.

Peg, Babs and I walked over to the nearest window. We tried to peer in but it was just too high. After a check of the rest of the windows it became obvious that everything low enough to look into was covered by a shade and only the higher windows were exposed. I'd taken the opportunity to examine the outside of the house and hadn't seen anything out of the ordinary, so I guessed there was nothing left for us to do.

"Okay, I guess this was kind of a dead end. We might as well head over to the office," I croaked despondently.

"Why?" asked Peg.

"Well, I think it's pretty clear that we've seen all we can and there's nothing to learn," I responded.

At that point Liv had finished with her phone call and was ready to join in the hunt.

"I'm ready," she declared.

"Too late," I countered.

As we bantered lightly about the disappointing dead end we'd hit, I noticed something out of the corner of my eye. Liv and I both watched as Peg and Babs hauled a humongous ladder out of the back of Peg's minivan.

"Oh no," we both yelled in unison.

Peg never batted an eyelash.

"Come on you two, help me get this up against that window."

Liv shot me a contrite look. She couldn't control them any better than I could. And if you can't beat 'em…

After looking through almost every window we were able to confirm very little. Our former colleague, Claire, had been a meticulous housekeeper. She'd been organized and neat almost to the point of obsession. Big surprise, she kept her home like she kept her office. Oddly, we never did find where there was any construction. We were hungry for some kind of clue but it was probably fruitless to think that there would be anything of note here that the police or her husband had failed to uncover. It was looking like a lost cause, not to mention a big waste of time. We were down to the last window. Babs and Liv hefted the ladder into place and Peg started her ascent. It was the back bedroom, the one Claire used for scrapbooking. As Peg reached the top of her climb, she let out a little squeal.

"Hey guys. I think we've got something here. This room has been trashed – it's a disaster. There's stuff all over the place. "

"Wait, let me see…"

"Come down here and let me take a look…"

Both Liv and I were anxious to get our turn at the window. God bless Babs, she's never impatient. After a few minutes of juggling we all got our turn viewing the carnage. We were all talking at once about what might have caused something like that when Babs calmly stated, "I wonder if he was after that envelope?"

"What envelope?" Liv clamored.

"Well, the one poking its little corner out from under the area rug. You can only see but one tiny little piece of it. I wonder if Claire had hidden some big secret and the killer trashed the room to find it before the cops did."

That led to another rush to the top of the ladder because naturally we all had to see for ourselves. Peg was the first one to regain her composure.

"So, here's what I think. I think we should open that window and grab that envelope."

"Are you crazy?" Liv retorted. "That's breaking and entering. There's prison time for that."

"Yeah," I quickly added. "I'm not doing time for Claire's sake under any circumstance."

"Oh pish tosh. I'll do it," said Peg as she stalwartly made her way back up the ladder.

The best attempts of each of us to coax her down were all in vain. When that woman makes up her mind there is no stopping her. We should not have been surprised.

At the top Peg placed one hand on each side of the window and pushed it up. No lock. She deftly stepped in through the open window as the three of us stared open mouthed at each other from below.

"I've got it," yelled Peg from inside Claire's craft bedroom.

And just as Peg placed her leg over the sill in preparation of her descent, a deafening blaring noise caused all of us to jump. Oh shit. Claire had had an alarm installed. Luckily when Peg jumped she was only half out of the window. She fell back into Claire's house with a resounding boom. But, that little Peg is quicker than you'd think. She scrambled out the window and practically slid down the ladder.

Liv and I had regained our composure enough that we both wheeled around at the same time – ready to bolt for the car. It was Babs and her pragmatic thinking - again - that stopped us in our tracks. No point in running. We'd never get the ladder loaded into the minivan in time. We'd most likely run into the security company AND the police on our way out of the neighborhood. Best to just stand here and wait.

She was right, as usual. Then, I started thinking about the remarkable presence of mind that both Babs and Peg had exhibited once the alarm had sounded. Just as the very thought occurred to me Liv barked, "Have you two done this before? How do you know so much about what to do?"

They were quick to assure us that neither had ever done any

B&E's before (That's breaking and entering to you honest, law abiding citizens). They explained that weird things come up when you're on location for a commercial shoot, and this didn't seem all that different frankly. Both Liv and I looked at them with wonder just as the entire emergency SWAT team pulled up to the curb.

Police and security jumped out and virtually leapt over to where we were standing. Leading the throng was Detective Warren, not looking particularly pleased to see us again.

"Oh god, what now?" she demanded incredulously. "Did you break into the vic's house?"

Peg stepped up.

"Of course not. We just wanted to take a look to see if something would jump out at us, so to speak. And by the way, did you know that the back bedroom has been ransacked?"

"What?" barked the good detective. "Simmons and Washburn, draw your weapons and check out that back bedroom. Are you sure you four didn't do this yourselves? We were just here yesterday and nothing had been touched."

"Absolutely sure, detective," I responded with my best "I'm as pure as the driven snow" look. To be honest, I probably should have practiced that look in the mirror before we attempted this caper. Based on the expression on Warren's face, it had been more like my "I just swallowed something disgusting and it's coming back up 'look'." Where's a mirror when you need one?

Once inside it was only moments before Simmons and Washburn confirmed that the vic's home had been breached. They also assured the rest of the team that the intruder did not appear to be on the premises. With that, the fearless entourage from law enforcement, Warren included, piled into Claire's house leaving the four of us to stand outside almost by ourselves. Apparently it occurred to all of us at about the same time that it might behoove us to make haste in packing up the ladder and getting ourselves out of there. Babs and Peg each grabbed a side of the ladder while Liv and I tried to figure out how to get it closed quickly. In the midst of the chaos, Peg couldn't resist sneaking a peak at the contents of the envelope; nothing…damn! With all of the distractions we had failed to notice a sergeant standing by, watching our every move. So it was a real surprise when he yelled out, "Back away from the ladder – now."

We jumped again. This time releasing our tentative hold on the ladder, which began a rapid descent of its own, landing right on top of said sergeant. He was out like a light. There appeared to be a fair amount of blood. Oops.

[CHAPTER 16]

Once we were released from the station house we headed back over to the office. Guess who we saw when the elevator doors opened.

"You guys are AWEsome!" Donny crowed. "I am having the BEST time.

It would be another long day.

"Hey Donny," I ventured "You're pretty quick to judge, but I don't see you sticking your neck out for the cause."

"Donna, I'm hurt," Donny cooed "I've risked the ire of Omaha's finest to prod and poke for information – and THIS is the thanks I get? That seems cold even for you."

All right, I had to give him that, but he could be so annoying sometimes. Especially when we knew we'd done something stupid.

"Hey," Donny continued. "I'll tell you what, if you schedule a review of the leads we have so far I'll, uh, help you analyze them. I'm sure I can get you further than you are now just by working through the evidence at hand."

Man he was cocky. It usually worked to our favor, but today it was getting on my last nerve.

"Oh really?" Liv chimed in before I had a chance to respond. "So you think you can out-analyze the four of us? Not on your best day Bucko."

Bucko? Where did that come from?

"I don't think, Miss 'let's just get this ladder out of here,' I know," preened Donny in all his self-righteous glory.

Oh god. I could see where this was going. We were about to split into two warring camps. An honest attempt to help solve a disturbing murder, disturbing because it struck so close to home, was about to become a Marcel competition. And the prize? Whichever group solved the murder got to feel superior over the other group until the next major competition came down the pike.

"Hey guys," I barked in order to stop the glarefest that always preceded a competitive challenge, "I'm not positive this is the best…"

Both team captains vehemently objected to my attempts to bring order back to impending chaos. There was no appealing to these two stubborn hotheads, each vying for the attention of the masses. They were at the starting gates and there was no stopping them, and there was no controlling them. I could see the thin veil of command that Kyle and I had garnered slip away into the mist as the clash of the titans began. I couldn't deny that it was an imposing sight. Liv was a tall statuesque woman standing over six feet in her heels, but Donny was significantly taller – he was a big guy. Standing in their faceoff poses, I was sure I could see smoke coming out of Donny's nostrils as they each continued to stare down their opponent. No one moved a muscle save for the rapid and agitated breathing.

After some reflection it occurred to me that this was probably the most productive way to harness their brainpower and get them to focus on the issue. They both loved competition. Oh, they never called it that – but every day was a constant challenge to see who could best the other in a very polite and seemingly civilized fashion. They weren't fooling any of us. We knew what drove them and we used it to our advantage for client challenges all the time.

In fact this would actually serve us in more than one way. Not only was their brainpower sure to be focused on the win and provide us with valuable insights, but their uncontrollable need to brag to non-team members in vivid detail was sure to provide me with a thorough, ongoing account of what each team had discovered. A competition would also keep them out of the way as Kyle and I continued our quest. As intelligent as they both were, their constant need to control everything could often burn valuable time as they moved to direct executions that were often already well underway and in need of no extra "managing." They weren't the only ones who could get things done, they just thought they were. Occasionally they would throw each other a grudging bone in order to maintain the peace, but they were often blissfully unaware of all the things that got accomplished around them. They were always appreciative after the fact, I'll give them that. Okay, at least Liv was.

I left Sugar Ray and Ali in their battle stances as I went in search of Kyle. As I headed around the corner I could hear them begin to

81

divvy up the team.

"I've got Lake," Liv growled.

"Fine, if I thought he knew anything I might be worried," Donny countered, trying to look unconcerned.

Donny was pretty predictable – nobody on the other team would be worth anything – until the next challenge when he snatched them up for his "dream team."

Once in Kyle's office it became evident that, as usual, he was already up to speed on the morning's excitement. News travels fast around here. "Kyle I…"

"Don't bother Donna, why just aggravate yourself more?" Kyle lamented. "Hey I've got something I know will interest you."

Why couldn't everyone be like Kyle? Always focused on the mission and not his own ego.

He continued "Guess who I'm having coffee with tomorrow morning? Claire's husband, the philandering DJ."

"No kidding?"

"You know I felt compelled to call him and express my condolences, and we got to talking. I got the feeling that things have been very weird for him, I mean, aside from the fact that his wife was brutally murdered. I don't think very many people have reached out to him. I got the definite impression that the people who didn't like her didn't make the effort. "

Yeah, that would be me. I felt my first real pang of guilt.

"And the others, the handful of people who liked her, were too angry about his affair to give him the time of day. He's definitely feeling a need to talk, and based on Claire's track record of alienation and destruction I might be his only option aside from his lady friend."

So typical of Kyle. Always taking the higher, kinder road he would undoubtedly make a genuine effort to lend support and care to the grieving widower. Like everyone else who talks to Kyle, I was sure that our wandering widower would spill his guts. Kyle just has that effect on people. He can put anyone at ease – and then they talk. It never fails.

"Do you think you'd want to join us, Donna?" asked Kyle.

"Are you kidding? With me there he'd seal up tighter than a space capsule before blastoff. No Kyle, we'll have a much better chance of getting the real skinny if it's just you two, but thanks for the offer."

"Oh Donna, I'm sure he'd be comfortable in front of you. You're incredibly good at getting people to talk yourself."

"That's very sweet of you Kyle, but that only applies to people I don't put on edge. And, I can assure you Claire's husband would be totally on edge with me there."

"Maybe you're right. Anyway I certainly wouldn't want to twist your arm – I'm more than happy to go solo on this one."

Kyle and I spent the next half hour making a list of issues that we felt would elicit the most meaningful information from our widower, Garth. We knew Kyle would have to play it by ear and see where the conversation went, he was a master at that, he could listen better than anyone. We just wanted to be sure that should the opportunity arise to dig around, he had a game plan in place. Odds were we wouldn't get another crack at this bird so we needed to hit it hard.

Once satisfied that all the bases were covered we took a few minutes to prepare a list of next steps. We made sure to include which issues we would surreptitiously try to foist on which of the "challenger" teams. When Liv and Donny were focused on the prize, you had to feed suggestions to them in a way that would make them think they arrived there all on their own. This wasn't hard to do.

For Donny's team we focused on police details and minutia as well as legal and financial issues surrounding Claire's burgeoning problems with work. For Liv, the topic would be centered around the various players, how they interacted and how that impacted others. She could analyze consumer patterns like nobody else!

The first item on our list was to find Lake and ask him about a recent talk he'd given on the five most common mistakes in digital marketing. We knew that many "persons of interest" for the murder had been scheduled to attend the event. We'd also heard it had been a huge success and had morphed into a big dinner and discussion group. That was pretty common for Lake. He had a brilliant command of his topic and in his quiet, unassuming way always blew people away once his knowledge and creativity were unveiled. In fact, the only person not completely convinced of his creativity was Lake – and Donny, when Lake was on Liv's team.

Kyle and I agreed to meet up again in a few hours to spend some time with Lake. He took off for his team meeting and I grabbed a power bar on my way to my new business materials review. If I kept skipping lunch this investigation might be good for my diet!

[CHAPTER 17]

At four, Kyle and I were able to corner Lake in the circular conference room.

"So Ross," Kyle started, "tell us all about your digital talk. We heard it went really well."

"Come on you guys. You can't kid me. I know you just want to hear what dirt I was able to pick up," brayed Lake in his "I've got your number" tone.

"Now Lake," I interceded, "think about who you're talking to. That might be true of me but no one could ever accuse Kyle of propping you up to pump you for information."

"True," Lake admitted. "I guess I lost my head for a second there. Do you really want to know about the talk?" he looked at Kyle.

"Ye…"

"No, not really," I shot back. "We want the dirt."

Lake spent the next 45 minutes telling us everything he'd learned. Some of it was a repetition of what we'd already unearthed

– with a slightly different spin in a few instances. There was, however, one additional piece of information that brought some clarity to Claire's office dilemma. One of her co-workers at Toto had been at Lake's talk. He'd dropped a few snarky comments about the deceased that went unnoticed by everyone but Lake, who'd heard that the guy was known as a chronic whiner who's comments often went unheeded.

As Lake proceeded to enlighten us it became evident that Claire's nefarious activities had included attempting to bribe the zoning commission. Apparently she'd become aware of a major national out-of-home buy coming into the market. Out-of-home is the official term we use for billboards and other various display media venues not found in the home. She wanted to find a way to make Toto, hands down, the most competitive company in the market since it had become clear that the buy was to be awarded to one company and one company only. Toto was just not as competitive out west as their major nemesis, Vox, but Claire thought she'd found the perfect solution: bribe a confidant on the zoning commission to allow Toto to build the two to four extra super bulletins in the vicinity out west that had thus far been denied them, or anyone else, by zoning law. With the extra boards Toto would be a shoo-in for the big buy. What Lake's information was not clear about was whether or not Claire was just doing this for self-aggrandizement and a modest bonus, or if she actually had a stake in the company. We thanked Lake and let him run to his 4:30 meeting. Since Kyle had to run himself, I made a beeline over to Donny's office. This news could be just the thing to jump start his team.

I got there just as Donny was heading out on a mission.

"Oh, I guess this is a bad time. You look like you're rushing," I observed.

"No, I don't have anything going on – this is a good time. What's up?" he inquired.

At these times I never knew if Donny was just being unusually nice or if he really had been about to charge around the agency with no particular goal in mind. And I'm guessing that was something I'd never know.

"We got some intelligence on the case and I wanted to see what you think about it." I slyly began, hoping my quarry would jump to the bait. "We've learned that Claire had actually tried to bribe someone on the zoning commission," I began.

Donny interrupted me, "You think that's new news?"

Here we go.

"My team has known that for a very long time now," he boasted. "In fact, I can tell you I've already solved this case. I know exactly what happened – and you know I'm never wrong about these things."

Oh yeah. We were off to a good start.

"Claire did try to bribe an acquaintance on the commission, someone she'd worked with at Fowler Mutual. Some of their correspondence got into the wrong hands and there was an investigation. Claire had made up her mind to throw the blame completely on her accomplice and make it appear as though she was just trying to help nab a crooked commission member. She didn't anticipate her pal's colossal panic attack as he faced the probability that his career would be over and he'd be blackballed from ever getting any more decent commissions. We're pretty sure that she goaded him on and he snapped."

That sure sounded like Claire.

"You mark my words, that's exactly how it happened. I've got this thing solved. " Donny crowed. "And Liv's team is over there trying to fit all the 'persons of interest' into generational groups to try and determine how they would respond to any given situation. She's even got Craig pulling stats on how they respond to various stimuli based on their demographics. What does she think we're doing here – promoting a movie? I'm telling you Donna, I've got this whole thing wrapped up."

"I'm not at all surprised, Donny," I cooed.

Craig was our data analytics guy in KC. He could slice and dice a target audience and fine tune their lifestyles and buying preferences like nobody's business. There were times we were sure it was more magic than data manipulation.

Donny took a moment to bask in the reflection of his self-satisfaction. I had to admit that he built an airtight case. It certainly made sense. But if he'd solved the case why hadn't he shared this information with his buddies on the force?

"So what did your old high school buddies have to say when you handed them the solved case all wrapped up in a nice, neat little bow?" I queried tentatively.

Donny's face darkened and tensed.

"They, uh, thought it was awesome," he garbled, "but they said there are some things they need to check on before handing it over to

Warren. They're just putzes really, I've always known that. Even in high school I had to drag them pretty far down the road before they'd get a clue and could wrap their Cro-Magnon heads around stuff. I'm used to it. It's always been a challenge getting them up to speed on anything."

"That's true, Donny," I jumped in "Most people cannot match your lightning fast ability to solve even the most complex of problems."

"Yeah, Donna. I love that you get me. And you just watch, those clowns will take my solution and track it down 'til they prove I'm right about everything. It shouldn't take them that long. Hell, it's so obvious even a moron like Lake could figure it out."

There it was. Lake was on Liv's team this time – so he remained a moron. You had to love that Donny. He could make the dullest day entertaining.

After my somewhat tiring chat with Donny I was feeling ready to head home and get a little R & R.

[CHAPTER 18]

I put on my right turn signal and turned in to my driveway.
It felt great to be home. As I walked through the door connecting
the garage to my house, I was greeted with the usual cacophony
of bulldog welcome. Gracie, my biggest Olde English Bulldogge,
weighing it at 95 pounds, pushed through with a dancing step,
swinging her big beautiful ears from side to side in a Dumbo-like
motion that told me she was happy Mom was home. Gracie was art
in motion. Her body moved like one of the large cats at the zoo and
she was attired in a glistening coat of pure white fur with coal black
spots. Her ears were large soft blankets of white and black trimmed
with a fringe of solid black. No artist could have created anything
more magnificent than this creature. She glided up close enough to
bump my knee with her nose and turned around to give Jasmine and
Roxi a chance to say hi to Mom.

Jasmine was my 85-pound Olde English Bulldogge. She had
a snow white head and a brown coat (although it's referred to as
red). Jasmine was lithe and athletic and moved like a deer. People

were fascinated with her one brown and one blue eye. She was my demure girl, very shy and tentative until you got to know her. Jasmine ran the house with her quiet command and she liked to make sure that we knew it. A feather touch of her delicate little nose and she gracefully moved away to find a toy to show me. The Olde English Bulldogge is a breed created as an attempt to bring the bulldog line closer to the original breed. They range in size between the English and the American bull. They also differ from the English bull by virtue of having a longer snout and a more natural mating and birthing capability. The Olde English is generally more athletic than the English bull – although no one's more athletic than my English Bulldog – Roxi.

Roxi was my only English Bulldog, weighing in at 65 pounds. She was on the large size – but still the baby of the family. Roxi sported a cream-colored coat as soft as a little bunny rabbit. On her coat were delicate brown spots, similar in color to Jasmine's. Her little cream and brown spotted ears resembled two butterflies perched next to her head, ready to lift her off to the treetops. Roxi was a scrapper. She knew how to make herself known. After a quick greeting, she turned to indicate that I was expected to scratch her butt. She was a very demanding little companion.

After a few minutes of circling and re-circling, the girls indicated that I had passed muster and was again welcome into the home. That was when I was able to look up and notice Jon for the first time. Jon was my husband of over thirty years, and he still looked like the dashing twenty-year-old I married.

Jon and I were very different. He was the quiet analytical type

91

and I was the human dynamo mowing down everything in my path. Somehow it seemed to work, and after all these years of sharing life, his very presence was enough to assure me that everything would be okay. That was my family.

"How was your day?" Jon started. He was attired in his usual jeans and button-down beachcomber shirt. For a number of years now Jon had officed out of the home, and it suited him. His life was his own, for the most part, with the possible exception of the occasional anxious client or more likely a very demanding canine. After thirty-plus years of marriage Jon still had the baby face and the handsome dark hair that had attracted me in the first place. Although friendly ribbing from friends would indicate that the face was not as baby-like and the hair was a tad thinner, I didn't see it.

"A little nuts."

"So, normal?"

"Pretty much. With the possible exception of a somewhat public mishap…"

"Read it on Facebook," he interrupted. His access to Facebook kept Jon apprised of the activities of Marcel and all of our employees.

"Figures."

Arriving at home after work I was often faced with comments from Jon along the lines of "Wow, Bridget really had a rough weekend, huh?" typically eliciting a blank, open mouthed stare from me. He would then proceed to fill me in on the strange and remarkable adventures of my co-workers.

"Found a few new pieces of information to add to our case," I added.

As sure as I was of my problem-solving brilliance I had to admit that it was usually Jon who came to the right conclusion before anyone else. His problem-solving skills were better than any I'd ever seen. I think Sherlock Holmes must have read books about Jon before setting out to solve any of his cases.

Reading murder mysteries was never much fun for Jon because he often identified the murderer within the first few pages. In our early years I thought he was making it up to try and look impressive. But after numerous occasions of having him write down the killer after ten pages – or ten minutes of a movie – I had to admit – Jon was amazing.

A few years ago I had the bright idea of spending New Year's Eve on a Murder Mystery boat trip down the Connecticut River. We actually had a lot of fun. The two of us were seated at a table with ten strangers. It was one of about thirty tables. We were given paper and pencils, and several scenes from a murder mystery were acted out in front of us. We were then instructed to work with our tablemates to solve the murder. Discussion began and took us in several different directions. We were all over the map and some of our less patient team members were starting to get a little heated in their oration – I think the alcohol contributed somewhat. After about twenty minutes of just listening, Jon started out quietly. He briefly outlined his conclusion. I could tell the group was about to turn from him when Jon very patiently began to detail the reasons behind his decision. One by one I could see our team members succumb to Jon's musings. At one point a big drunken bully at the end of the table tried to regain the attention and was resoundingly silenced - and none too politely. There was my Jon, in his quiet, unassuming way capturing the loyalty of all these strangers. Once he finished no one spoke a word in disagreement. It was decided that Jon's conclusions would be our official answer so we called the judge over.

As we waited for the judge to arrive at our table, I could see that the rest of the tables were in an uproar. No one was even close to reaching any kind of agreement. After listening to our solution, the judge just shook his head.

"Looks like we have a winner," he declared.

We were asked to share our solution with all three hundred-plus revelers. Jon was happy to leave that honor to a guy with a ton of nervous energy who'd come up with about ten solutions himself – none of them close. After parroting Jon's solution, verbatim, Mr. Nervous took us to a shining victory! In fact, our table was the big winner of the night.

Much to my amusement we were visited by a steady stream of well wishers who wanted to share the fact that they had not even been close. By the end of the evening I realized that my husband was the only attendee who'd solved the problem, and in record time. I wasn't at all surprised!

I was glad Jon had solved the puzzle so quickly. It left us more time to dance and the music had been great!

I figured Jon would crack the case before anyone else.

I moved to the kitchen to pour a glass of my favorite Sauvignon Blanc from my own little wine fridge in the kitchen over the TrashMasher. Jon has three formidable wine fridges downstairs in the bar and whenever I'd find myself home alone and eager for a relaxing glass of wine, I'd peruse his collection for the perfect choice and invariably end up with a tumbler of Crystal Lite. It's very intimidating. I never knew which bottle to open. Is this too expensive? Will I like this one? Is he saving this for a special occasion? That never happens now! Mmmmm I could tell that Jon had been busy in the kitchen himself.

"That smells great," I blurted as I moved to the stove to identify the culinary delight that was assailing my senses.

"I know things have been a little tense for the past few days and I thought you could use a treat. So I whipped up a little shrimp scampi over linguini. Hope you don't mind skipping your diet for one night."

"Perfect!"

That man could definitely read my mind. I had been dreading the thought of cutting up my veggies and heating up my NutriSystem dinner in my fervor to shed those last seven pounds. Normally I kind of enjoyed the discipline and there were actually some dinners that tasted pretty good, but being pampered with a gourmet meal was unquestionably a better proposition considering my mood and level of exhaustion. I sat down, closed my eyes and sniffed a delicate and fruity, but not really sweet, bouquet. This would be good.

We had a wonderful, relaxing meal as we discussed the events of the day. As usual, when all was said and done it was Jon who was giving me information. He'd pretty much known everything that I knew either from chatting with colleagues and acquaintances or from Facebook and Twitter updates.

"Just being Facebook 'friends' with Clovis alone is a wealth of information that makes all the rest of her assaults on your sensibilities worthwhile. You should 'friend' her," he offered.

"Oh hell no, I can't imagine any information that would make being subjected to her on an ongoing basis worthwhile. You're just a stronger person than I, and besides, how do you know that anything she puts out there is true and not just a figment of some hideously twisted imagination?"

"Good point. You have to do some sifting," he acknowledged. "It wasn't tough to figure when she said she was on a 'sort of' date with Claire's husband the night of the murder – and I realized what that really meant was that his station had sponsored a dinner for their five hundred closest friends that night and he was the emcee – well, you know Clovis."

Yes, unfortunately I did know Clovis. God help me, I did.

This seemed like the perfect time to change the subject. We cleaned up the dinner dishes and gave our girls their favorite liver treats. Then we all went down to watch an old movie on Jon's seventy inch TV. It was a lovely, relaxing and altogether satisfying evening, the concluding details of which will be left to your own imagination.

[CHAPTER 19]

Back in the office the next morning I was pacing like a caged tiger. Why had I declined coffee with Kyle and "the Hubby" again? Curiosity was driving me crazy!

"Hey Donna, did you get a chance to review that brochure copy that I left on your desk last night?" Peg urged: "You know we're trying to get to press before noon."

"Okay, yeah, I'm almost done," I fibbed.

She was right – I had to focus, but it was so hard to read and reread copy looking for any little necessary change when you were too antsy to sit still for two minutes. Also, my office was like a damn greenhouse. I couldn't even blame it on menopause, at least not completely. The offices along the south side of the building were brutal in the morning sun. I was fortunate enough to have a full bank of windows from the ceiling to about waist level and I absolutely reveled in the glorious sunlight – but damned if it didn't make me sweat like a sumo wrestler trapped in a steam room when I first got in every morning. Anytime someone would come to speak with me about a more private issue they would look around furtively. My suggestion that we might want to close the door would generally be met with an anguished cry of, "No, please, not that, if you close the door I will suffocate." Yeah, how do you think I feel. Colleagues would actually come into my office to "warm up" on some of those colder mornings. It was extreme.

By the time I had finished getting my comments on the brochure copy back to Peg and writing my next blog for the 'Insights' section of our website my phone started to ring. I could see it was Kyle's cell.

"Hey where are you?"

"I'm still at the coffee place near Dodge and 114th Street. Do you think you could run out here for a minute? I could use another cup of coffee and I'd rather fill you in without interruption," Kyle pleaded.

"Sure, give me a sec, I'll be right out," I hurriedly agreed.

Hell, it was a gorgeous day. I wouldn't mind escaping for a bit. Besides my head was getting a little foggy, so I could use a nice break.

As it was still too chilly to sit al fresco, Kyle waited inside at the table closest to the window, sipping his mocha latte grande with a dazed look on his face. He barely noticed me as I passed by to order my double hazelnut with a shot of espresso. This was going to be interesting.

"Donna, is there such a thing as too much compassion?" Kyle began. "I know my wife, Lori, would probably tell me to look in the mirror but honestly, Donna, can it go too far?"

"In your case, Kyle, I'd have to side with Lori. Not that she's all that far behind you herself," I offered. They were about the two sweetest people I knew.

Kyle was clearly hurting. He looked almost torn. I hated to see him like this.

"Kyle, what did he tell you?" I beseeched him. He was starting to give me some discomfort.

He sighed – a big long sigh. Then he started.

"Donna, I think Garth is having a mental breakdown. I think it's guilt that he honestly didn't have any feelings for her anymore. He was just sticking it out because of the boy, and on top of that he really felt guilty about his extramarital activities. He says he's not the philandering type and I believe him. Oh, and he also said that he didn't kill Claire. I believe that too."

"Wow, Kyle you two really clicked, huh?"

"He was just so grateful to have someone to confide in. Seems as though he needed to open up to some one. He doesn't feel comfortable sharing details of his life with Claire with his enamorata. They'd always tried to keep his family business out of their relationship, and now she's pushing for something more permanent. He's really torn."

"That is pretty heavy. So he really doesn't care for what's her name?"

"Lacy," Kyle offered. "No it's not that he doesn't care for her, he's just not in a good place emotionally so he doesn't want to make any promises until he gets his head back on straight. He also has to consider his son and how something like this would affect him." Kyle could totally get that. He and Lori had two boys and a girl and

99

they were devoted parents who would never take a step without considering the welfare of all three.

"Sounds like he's thinking better than he gives himself credit for," I rejoined.

"Oh, in many ways he is. He's a very smart guy. He's also starting to see the logic in not getting involved with a co-worker. I guess things are pretty intense over there."

"Well that's kind of the first thing they teach you in business, isn't it?" I pushed.

"That's true. But from what he told me, this thing just took them both by surprise. It's not something they'd planned. He seemed very introspective when he said that he and Claire had been moving apart. She'd been acting furtive and secretive, and he'd been lonely, so he was vulnerable when the charming and lovely new LSM started at the station. She clearly wanted his attention and despite his best efforts to stave off her advances, he couldn't help but feel flattered that a beautiful, intelligent young woman in his industry found him exciting – when he'd been feeling as though those days were long gone. He doesn't try to justify his actions, and believe me he's beating himself up pretty badly over the whole thing."

"Yeah, I always thought Garth was a decent guy. Felt sorry for him getting hooked up with such a shrewish hag," I agreed.

Kyle laughed. "You know, Donna, if you'd said that about anyone else I'd be giving you a piece of my mind right now. But in Claire's case I think you're being too kind."

"Well, this is all very interesting, Kyle, but it doesn't explain why you seem so rattled. Am I wrong or is there something else I haven't heard yet?" I pushed further.

"Right as usual, Donna," Kyle responded sheepishly. "For me, the worst part is that in Garth's estimation everything started to go wrong for Claire from the minute she left Marcel, and I just can't shake the guilt over the fact that I was one of the ones who was anxious for her to go."

"Well what the hell does he mean by that anyway?" I bellowed. At that point the people at the two tables near us decided it was time to go. "Oh shit, maybe I should take it down a notch or two." We "ad" people can be notoriously emotive. Even the most buttoned down of us would have had trouble making it in the corporate/ banker-subdued environment that many of our clients lived in. We wore our hearts on our sleeves, and that was not always a good thing.

"Is he trying to suggest that we…" I continued in a far more subdued voice, kind of like I thought one of my clients would converse with a colleague.

"No, no, no," Kyle interrupted before I'd gotten too far. "He's not trying to insinuate anything. He was just saying that when she left Marcel she seemed to lose her inner compass. She, um, kind of lost her ability to tell right from wrong."

"Because, hell, she landed herself a nice gig making a damn good salary, I've heard," I interjected.

"Yes, that's true. At first it seemed as though things would go well for her. But shortly after starting her new job she started to panic and wanted back into Marcel. Don't you remember that Liv got calls from a number of contacts telling her that they'd heard Claire was coming back?"

"I certainly do remember that, and it would have happened over all of our dead bodies!" I bellowed. There I go again – I saw the coffee barista look up in surprise. Cool it Donna. How embarrassing would it be to get thrown out of Starbuck's for loud and disorderly conduct? I could tell I was starting to make Kyle uncomfortable.

"Hey Donna do you want to finish this conversation back at the office?" he chimed in hastily.

"I'm sorry Kyle, but you know how terrifying a notion that was to me. If I were a cat I'd have used up three lives over that scare alone. If you recall, we were nervous that some of the clients would push to get her back." I could feel myself start to shiver at the recollection alone.

"I remember well. I also remember how relieved we were to learn, one by one, that the clients couldn't stand her either. Then, we felt stupid for letting her stay as long as we had," Kyle offered. "No, Donna, Garth was really making more of an observation than anything. It was his way of explaining how things started to unravel. Once they started it was zero to 60 in a heartbeat. He said he saw it happening before his eyes but he felt helpless to stop the downhill slide. "

"Well, I guess I'm still not sure what did happen," I ventured.

"Oh, it was a whole lot," Kyle continued. "She pushed to be made an owner of Toto assuming they would be thrilled to share their business with the great Claire. She'd started thinking of herself as a cross between Bill Gates and Warren Buffett. But, Claire was the only one who saw herself that way. The owner of Toto told her that he would consider allowing her to buy into the company if she were to make her mark in their industry in a meaningful way – and in particular, a way that would be beneficial to his company."

"Well that certainly gave her a lot of latitude," I commented.

"Yes, but you must realize that the great and powerful Claire was stunned that they even thought of making her buy her way in. She expected to be welcomed into the ownership circle with open arms – sans cash."

"Well what business operates that way?" I growled. "That's just ridiculous."

"Correct, but when you're a home-grown talent who's been allowed to see yourself as a brilliant and innovative thinker, you've basically taken your already overblown ego, added Miracle-Gro and stuck it in a new pot the size of the Superdome! There would be no stopping you, and the usual business practices would not apply," Kyle asserted.

I had to concur. It sounded just like Claire, and I felt a pang of guilt that we had, in any way, contributed to the care and feeding of the Godzilla-sized ego set loose on the innocent citizens of Omaha. I guess there was a lot of guilt going around these days.

"So what happened?" I pressed. This was starting to get a bit surreal.

"Um, well, that's where Garth was not absolutely on solid ground," Kyle faltered. "He thinks she concocted a brilliant plan to do what her future partner had been "too wimpy" (in Claire's own words to Garth) to accomplish. He thinks the plan included bribery of a zoning official who was a former co-worker of Claire's.

He sensed that she felt above recrimination and she scoffed at the seriousness of her intended offense."

At this point my eyebrows had about reached my hairline. I was speechless and you have no idea how difficult that is to achieve.

"And," Kyle continued, "it appeared as though Claire was going to get away with her scheme unscathed – unrewarded but unscathed – when a problem arose. Word on the street is that Toto had been dabbling in some money laundering prior to Claire's joining the company. As a result, the feds had planted a mole in the company. The mole got wind of Claire's nefarious doings and things started to fall apart at an alarming rate."

I was on the edge of my seat.

"So what happened next?" I pleaded. "Don't leave me in suspense!"

"Well, that's where it gets a little fuzzy. Garth isn't sure if there were more bribes, and if there were he isn't sure whether they were made on behalf of the money launderers or Claire. No one at Toto was trusting anyone, and everyone was gearing up for a counterattack. At this point Claire hadn't confided in Garth for a very long time. He was embarrassed to admit that he found all this out by going through e-mails on her g-mail account after her death."

"Holy crap, Kyle."

"Yeah, holy crap," Kyle repeated. "I've got a meeting in three minutes."

We bolted back to the office, Kyle for his 11:00 conference call and me to finish that damn blog before Liv came and beat me with a stick. Oh great, the brochure was back on my desk for one last check before our noon deadline. Good luck getting me to concentrate. I was like a cat on a hot tin roof! I wanted to share all of this with someone – but who? Maybe if I played my cards right I could get Liv to grab a Subway sandwich with me over lunch. I knew it was a long shot – she never had time for lunch. But I knew this would interest her and I was dying to find out what her data analysis had pointed out. Hell, I'd give it a shot.

[CHAPTER 20]

I placed a quick call to Jon to tell him that I doubted I'd be home for lunch. When you're on a diet it's just easier to go home for meals rather than lugging all of your fruits and veggies to the office.

"I figured it out," he stated quietly.

"Figured what out?" I demanded. No time for riddles.

"Who killed Claire," he answered matter-of-factly.

"What?" I yammered dully.

"I figured out who killed Claire," he repeated.

"What, who?" I demanded urgently.

"I don't have all the details worked out yet so I'm not quite ready to share," he countered. "But I'll write it down on a piece of paper and seal it in an envelope. Then, when I'm ready, or when the police figure it out, you can see if I was right."

Here we go again.

"Any hints?" I weaseled.

"Not yet," he teased.

You'll have to admit that sometimes I was a saint!

I called Liv to check on her lunch availability. She suggested we invite Melissa and Shelly to join us. Neither one was particularly fond of Claire, and they were both solid thinkers who might well have stumbled upon some intelligence that we'd missed. I agreed that the four of us should confab over lunch so I set it up. Melissa and Shelly had been roommates in college. After Melissa had been at Marcel for a couple of years, a position opened up that enabled her to achieve two major goals: find us an experienced and talented account manager and bring her pal, Shelly, back from the southeast. It was a great solution all the way around. The added benefit was that when you were around Melissa and Shelly you couldn't help but have a fabulous time. They were fun and funny, hip and razor sharp and they dressed in a lively and funky but very professional style. Just the type of people that flourished at Marcel.

With a foursome for lunch we decided to upgrade to Hector's, a Mexican restaurant with great margarita's and even better fajitas. So much for the diet. We sat in our plush red booth among the earth-toned walls strewn with festive ponchos and Mexican straw hats adorning their roughly textured surfaces. Our booth was across from the massive bar suited more to the happy hour crowd than the business lunch crew like us. After our first margarita it was time to get down to business. I filled Mel and Shell in on the status of the investigation. Having worked with Clovis they were alternately groaning and laughing at her predictable antics. Then, Shell commented, "I was surprised to see Bat in the office last week."

"When last week?" I mused.

Bat was Clovis' on-again, off- again freak of a boyfriend. When

107

they were on, he was handsome, brilliant and the most successful businessman in the entire market. No one else had a husband or boyfriend who could shine his shoes. When they were off, he was a sleazy bum who rode his cycle to work because he couldn't afford a running car and couldn't afford to buy her jewelry retail which is why she claimed he frequented the local pawn shops. On his own we'd observed that Bat was a nut job – perfect for Clovis, but problematic anywhere else. We all dreaded those on-again moments when he was dragged along to all of our functions. His erratic motions and jerky speech pattern made him difficult to be around, and at all times his demeanor hinted at potential Vesuvius behavior, not someone you were likely to relax around under any circumstances. It was surprising to hear that he'd been in the office since Clovis hadn't worked there for over six months.

"I think late in the week, I'm not sure," Shell responded. "He said Clovis had left some books that she just realized she needed."

"That's bull," I commented vehemently. "I don't think they're even together right now."

"Yeah, we knew that when we heard it," Mel quipped. "But who'd want to piss him off? He's such a freak."

At that point the conversation turned to Clovis and her recent trials and tribulations. According to Mel she was all kinds of irritated that the widower turned out to be hot for someone other than her. She'd been working hard to concoct a scenario where Garth had actually been using Lacy in order to get to her. But even she knew that it wasn't holding water. That's a bad day for Clovis.

Shell pointed out that Clovis had sat with Claire at the Boy Scout dinner. She'd left for the ladies' room right before the end and no one saw her again after that. There was some real speculation on the street that Clovis was the one who dealt the fatal blow. Since the police haven't released details reconstructing the crime there's no way of knowing if Clovis could physically have caused this murder. It would be pretty easy to rule her out if the forensic evidence indicated that she would not have the strength or stature to commit the crime. We would love to have known.

Just as we were ready to move on to another murder-related topic, who should walk into Hector's but Clovis. Oh god!

"Ladies," she crowed, "You were talking about me weren't you? Don't deny it now, I can tell."

"Clovis," Liv crooned, "You know we'd never talk about you behind your back."

Nice try Liv. Right comeback but with a delay of two seconds too long she wasn't buying it. We were sunk.

"Now girls," Clovis continued, "I know you've got my back. I know you'll be there for me right up until the end. After all, we were a team weren't we?"

She finished to half-hearted acknowledgments from all four of us. What choice did we have? We'd been caught in the act – there was a price to pay. And I had a sinking feeling it would be a hefty one. Oh yeah, there would be some serious pain in the payback for this regrettable indiscretion.

"Let me tell you what I need you to do," she commanded.

This would not be good. The next five minutes passed like an hour while we listened to Clovis' demands. Basically she wanted us to meet with everyone else who sat at her table the night of the Boy Scout dinner. She wanted to know what they thought had happened and what they thought of Clovis' involvement. In retrospect it was probably something we should have been doing anyway so we agreed fairly quickly. Before she left, Clovis left no doubt in any of our minds that her main objective, though she claimed to want vindication, was to ensure that as many people would continue to talk about her for as long as possible. Fascinating, really. I think she would rather be convicted of murder than to have people stop talking about her.

And as her "coup de grace" she managed to get a shot in about Mel and Shell. She made it clear that neither would succeed in "finding a man" without her dedicated support. There was even a barely concealed implication that only she could attract the opposite sex, so she would be forced to selflessly lend herself out as bait for these less fortunate compadres. The fact that both Mel and Shell were currently in healthy, long term relationships was inconsequential to her.

After she left we felt as though we'd really dodged a bullet. Between us we each selected two of her table companions to interview – it was a table for 10 and with Claire dead and Clovis as our "client" that left us with 8 people to approach. It seemed the best way to skin this cat. Anyway Liv knew two of them and Mel knew another one. Shell and I each took two strangers. We spent the rest of lunch devising questions to ask each of them. It would be tricky to question strangers without having them think they were under investigation themselves. Best not to anger anyone – who knows which, if any of them, had murdered Claire. We made a pact not to see any of the "tablemates" in person and alone –why take unnecessary chances.

After lunch we headed back to the office. We had some work to do. Before we pulled into the drive Mel remembered that the guy she knew had a home office nearby. She thought it best for the four of us to visit him all at once. Then we could see his physical reaction to the questions – but there would be safety in numbers. So we headed to Bob Stevens' home office.

Bob seemed more than a little surprised to see Mel and three women he didn't know. Naturally he recognized Liv from a speaking engagement she had given on social media. It was entitled "Facebook, it can help or it can really hurt you. Know how to use it."

"Hi Mel, what's up?" Bob queried tentatively without taking his eyes off of the three of us. "Oh hi, you're that social media expert," he directed at Liv. "I enjoyed hearing you speak at the Qwest Center."

"Thanks," Liv responded.

"Hi Bob," Mel began. "We're just heading back to the office from lunch and I remembered that you were at Claire's table "that night." You can imagine we're all really anxious to see this thing get solved, what with Claire having been one of our co-workers for so long. We thought you might know something we hadn't heard."

"Oh right," Bob countered thoughtfully. "I'd forgotten that she used to work at Marcel. Well, I talked to the police that night and answered all of their questions. I got the feeling from them that I didn't really know anything worth hearing."

"You know how they can be, I mean from watching TV

detectives, they try to keep things as close to the vest as possible. So they wouldn't really let on if you said something of interest," Mel pointed out knowingly.

"Yeah, I know what happens on TV," Bob continued. "But the cop who questioned me was my younger brother's best friend from grade school, Jimmy. Believe me, I could always read that kid like an open book. No, I didn't have anything that interested him at all, and trust me, I'd know."

"Good point," Mel concurred. "So just for the hell of it, what did you tell him?"

"Well," Bob began again, "I mentioned that Claire acted like a 'cat on a hot tin roof' all evening. But, of course, everyone knew she was skating on thin ice at her job so there was reason for her nervousness, and we also thought she was anxious for her son 'cause he was being honored with the other newly promoted Scouts. "

"Claire having trouble at work?" I pondered, having trouble concentrating on what Bob had to say, "How am I always the last to know?"

"That's all?" Mel interrupted impatiently bringing my attention back to the present.

I shot her a look. She should know that pushing a witness was the best way to get them to clam up. But I guess she didn't have the benefit of my interrogation experience- all those years of conducting primary research were clearly paying off for me - so I gave her the leeway to handle things as she saw fit, and her next comment made it clear that my "look" had not gone unnoticed.

"I mean, take all the time you need, Bob. What else did you

observe?" she continued more solicitously.

"There wasn't too much more." Bob offered, "It was a pretty routine rubber chicken dinner."

We waited. I held my breath hoping that Mel would make use of the pregnant pause. She did.

"Well, now that I think of it," Bob continued, "Claire's phone vibrated during the salad, and when she saw who was calling she went white."

Now we were getting somewhere.

"At first it seemed as though she was going to try to ignore it," Bob chirped, picking up steam as his memory improved. "But then she rushed off. We thought she was going to call the person back but I don't think that's what she did."

"What do you mean?" Liv and I both asked at once.

"Well," Bob continued, shooting us an indignant look for interrupting his memory breakthrough. "It appeared as though she was going into the hall to take that phone call, but I think she actually went outside and had her meeting in person."

"Why?" we all shouted.

Now Bob was on a roll. I guessed that he was not used to getting any attention at all and now he had four attractive, intelligent women hanging on his every word. Bob had no intention of rushing his moment.

"Weellll," Bob dragged on, "the way I figure it, she wanted us to think she was having a call in the hallway 'cause that's what she said when she got back. But, I noticed that she had huge goosebumps on her arms – it was unseasonably cold that night - and her hair was all

113

disheveled like from the wind, so I'm pretty sure she'd been outside. Why go outside to return a call when there were plenty of quiet empty hallways in the building? Yeah, I'd have to say she'd been outside meeting with someone who didn't want to be seen inside."

He paused and we all stood there like dummies. Shell finally regained her composure.

"Did you tell this to Jimmy?" Shell questioned anxiously.

"You know, I have to admit I didn't," he offered sheepishly. "I guess I just didn't think of it. Do you think she was meeting with the murderer?"

"It's certainly a distinct possibility," I chimed in, confident that we'd gotten the most we were going to get out of this witness. "Oh yeah," I continued, "do you think it could have been Clovis?" I asked not expecting a positive response but with the express purpose of being able to get Clovis off of all of our backs – for the moment anyway.

"I don't know," he responded. "Clovis spent the whole night running back and forth to the ladies' room in tears," he stated bemusedly.

"Why?" I asked. Man I wasn't expecting that. Bob thought Clovis might have been the killer. I was half listening to his response and half wondering what the hell we would tell Clovis to keep her from going completely postal. Although truth be told, running back and forth to the ladies' room in tears was pretty much *de rigeur* for Clovis in her "dramas R us" world. It was just that this time it could be the thing that made her a bona fide murder suspect.

Bob pressed on. "Oh let's see, she saw her off-again beau and he looked at her indifferently. Then she saw... I think she saw her old boss, and he said they missed her at work. Well, she could certainly understand how miserable she'd made them all by leaving, " Bob mused slipping into full sarcasm at this point – Clovis strikes again! "And what else? Oh yeah, I think she was expecting to be called onto the stage to speak extemporaneously because one of the Scouts honored was a friend of her son's and she was sure that she'd be named the most valuable influence in his life."

Bob was starting to enjoy this too much.

"Okay Bob," Liv interceded. "We get it. It was a typical night for Clovis. All me, all the time. Nothing out of the ordinary."

"Right," Bob agreed. "But she was away from the table during the 'mystery' meeting. So assuming that the meeting took place with the murderer..."

"Whoa, whoa, we're making way too many assumptions here," I jumped in. "I mean there's really no way of knowing any of these things. We need to just keep gathering information and let the facts form their own conclusion. If we keep trying to make the pieces fit, we won't recognize the truth when it's ready to come up and bite us in the face."

"That was a bizarre metaphor," Liv piped up, "but you're absolutely right. Ironically, that was one of the things that always drove me nuts about Claire. She started with a few assumptions and before the research was conducted she'd wrapped them all in a nice neat bow and document all of her conclusions. I used to always tell her to wait and let the facts speak for themselves – research is about finding the truth. But she was so determined that her logic was flawless that she would be shocked when the results did not support her conclusions. "

"I remember," I added, "when results of the research would come in and nothing would fit together, you'd always have to help her grudgingly shift gears. She valued logic over truth. I bet they put that on her headstone."

Liv shuddered visibly. Yeah, I always took things a step too far for her comfort. It was time to get going.

"Hey Bob, thanks for the info," Mel said taking the conversation firmly back in hand. "Maybe you should call Jimmy and fill him in on what you remember."

"Yeah, I will." We heard Bob respond as we walked out of the door and back to the car.

[CHAPTER 21]

Back at the office we all scrambled to get to our offices and get caught up on our work for the day. After about three hours of solid hustle I was ready to give some thought to the investigation. I contemplated my two anticipated witness interviews with some trepidation. It was a pretty awkward thing to call two strangers and push them for information on an incredibly sensitive topic for which I technically had no official reason to be involved.

It occurred to me that the best solution to this dilemma would be to find someone who knew these individuals and use them as a conduit. So, I started to think. I knew one of my witnesses had worked at Marred, a small local ad agency. Hmmm. Kyle had worked at Marred years ago – I wondered if they knew each other. I jotted down Cindy and Kyle – worth exploring. The other witness, Jarrod, was a member of PRSA, the firm for public relations professionals. I figured good old Sutter could help me out there. I checked Kyle's office – empty. He was undoubtedly in one of his numerous client meetings, but I was in luck – Sutter was in his office plugging away at a technical article for the education of architects. Loathe to interrupt his diligence I finally determined that solving a brutal slaying trumped educating architects – by a hair.

I cleared my throat. "Excuse me, Sutter," I began.

Tim looked up and I proceeded to give him the story I had concocted to enlist his aid with Jarrod. It was immediately clear that he had more than a passing acquaintance with my witness. They had bonded when covering last year's College World Series together. Sutter, as the chief publicist for our CWS client, and Jarrod, as the sports reporter for the local daily newspaper. Good to know. I would have to be more clever than ever in my subterfuge. Sutter was a straight shooter and would never willingly get in the middle of an ongoing police investigation. If he even had a clue as to what I was doing he'd clam right up. Not to mention the fact that, if he considered Jarrod to be a "comrade in arms" I stood no chance of getting a peep out of him. Sutter was more loyal than a bloodhound. He stood by his friends stalwartly and never caved. Sutter was the guy you wanted on your side in a pinch, but not so much when you were looking for a little gossip involving one of his homies.

I carefully explained that I wanted to talk to Jarrod about his recent column that featured the New York Yankees. Sutter knew that my husband was a huge fan so I figured he'd buy my cover. I went on to explain that, since Jarrod was somewhat of a local celebrity I wanted to mention Sutter's name when I contacted him so he wouldn't be so quick to brush me off. Sutter seemed to buy that too, so he gave me Jarrod's phone number and a few pointers.

"Don't mention his column on game five from last year. He

totally downplayed a blown call and he's been taking heat over it for the whole year," Sutter cautioned.

Not a problem since I had no idea who even played the fifth game last year. Sutter was giving me far more credit than was due, but I listened attentively.

"Oh, and he's particularly proud of his column on the last game last year. Everybody tells him he summed up 'the feeling' better than Howard Cosell ever did in his whole career. It was a big coup for him," Sutter advised.

Once he felt I had the high points, Sutter cheerily sent me on my way. I hated being less than perfectly honest with him, but it was for the greater good.

Back at the desk I dialed Jarrod's number and waited.

"Carmichael here," Jarrod answered at last.

"Oh hi, Jarrod" I began. "You don't know me but I work with Tim Sutter."

"How is good old Sutter?" Jarrod eased into a comfortable tone.

"Oh Tim's great, as usual," I replied. "He gave me your number because I had a few sports questions I wanted to ask you."

I garbled my way through a handful of sports questions as best I could. Luckily I was able to plead ignorance, and trust me that was easy, but profess a need to inform my sports fanatic husband. All true – so fairly plausible, except for the part that I cared about any of the answers to these questions. After we'd chatted for a few minutes I figured he was ready for the main course.

"So Jarrod," I treaded lightly, "I heard someone say you were at Claire's table the night of…"

"Yeah, you heard right," he responded a bit more curtly.

Better be careful. This could be a hostile one.

"Wow, that must have been weird to sit and have dinner with a person and then find out the next day that they were dead, huh?" I floated holding my breath.

"I guess," he mumbled. "Can't say it's ever happened to me before. But I should probably be getting back to my column."

"I guess Clovis was kind of annoying that night," I pressed hopefully.

"Who? Uh oh, you mean the scrawny blond? Downright bizarre if you ask me."

"I'd heard she did a lot of crying and running back and forth. Sounds pretty distracting," I offered.

"Not just distracting," he eased into his assessment of Clovis' behavior. "She scared the hell out of me."

"Scared, like in, she had a weapon and you thought she'd hurt you?" I pushed dying of curiosity.

"Nah, nothin' like that," he assured me. "She said she hoped it was okay if she put her hand in mine while we talked because she saw her boyfriend across the room and wanted to make him angry. What am I, an idiot? I'm not about to get in the middle of a scene like that. She was a freak show. So I spent a major portion of the night pushing her hands away from me."

Oh god, Clovis, no wonder you need to recon on what people are saying about you. As usual you've supplied them with an endless array of bizarre possibilities for speculation.

We spent the next few minutes chatting about the fact that even the bizarreness of her request to him that night was merely the tip of the iceberg for Clovis intimates. He hadn't seen nothin' yet. I did assure him, however, that now that he was on her list of "personal friends" he'd not seen the last of Clovis and her bizarre requests.

Jarrod groaned. I believe he was in actual pain. Another Clovis-related casualty. Then he said something that got me back on focus.

"Yeah, you could tell Claire couldn't tolerate her," he remarked. "Clovis had asked Claire to go out for coffee after the dinner and Claire lost no time in assuring Clovis that she was expecting someone and they planned to go out for a drink."

I was speechless.

"Hey Jarrod," I tried to sound casual, "Did you ever mention that to the police?"

"You know, now that you mention it I'd forgotten that until just now," he replied sheepishly. "Kind of embarrassing for a reporter to admit, huh? Maybe I'd better give them a call now."

We hung up and I just sat there trying to make sense of this new piece of information. Who could she have been meeting? I tried to get it out of Jarrod but he was either too embarrassed or he really couldn't remember. Was her mysterious rendezvous with the killer, or could that person be a terrified witness to the murder? All in all I thought it had been a very productive call.

[CHAPTER 22]

Next, I raced over to Donny's office. I wanted him on the case
of the mystery drink date tout suite. Donny immediately saw this as
an opportunity to jump ahead of Liv and her team so he was off to
the races. He would coordinate with his high school buddies/cops
and get to the bottom of what could be a crucial lead – either working
with them or just ahead of them. Luckily his pals never seemed to
resent Donny's ability to figure out the facts of any case and present
them with a laudable solution. Hell, it always ended up making
them look good in the department.

I felt positive about leaving that trail with a hungry wolf on the
scent.

On to step two, finding Kyle and getting connected to Cindy.
Luckily this time Kyle was in his office answering a few last minute
e-mails. So I filled him in on my day. He agreed that getting
to Cindy was a good idea. He did kind of get stuck on Jarrod's
horrifyingly embarrassing account of Clovis' dinner behavior, for
just a second though. After relaying the whole story to him I had to

give him a moment to stop, stare straight ahead in shock and wonder, shake his head a few times, murmur under his breath and then return to quasi-normal in order to tune back in to our conversation.

"Donna," he started.

"No exaggeration, Kyle," I headed him off at the pass.

"I'm stunned," he muttered, "and I honestly thought that was impossible, I thought nothing about her could shock me. I'm so very relieved that I wasn't there to witness it myself. I'm not sure I would have survived."

Kyle was a model of decorum and Clovis' junior high antics were beyond belief for him. He sat for another moment before starting to really come around. Then we began discussing our game plan for Cindy, and mistakenly I thought that this maneuver might prove to be more sane than the last several.

Why didn't it surprise me that, as with everything else connected to this murder investigation, we were about to embark on yet another twisted adventure. Although we realized it then, we had no idea just how twisted things would get.

As Kyle began to inform me of Cindy and her unusual lifestyle it dawned on me that we were headed down the rapids without a life preserver, so it was best to just hold our breath and ride it out.

Apparently Cindy and her significant other, Carl, were body builders and professional wrestlers. Working at an ad agency was just a way to put food on her table and support her one true love – her body and its ability to inflict harm on other bodies. Yippee!

To make matters more interesting, Kyle pointed out that Cindy did not own a phone and would not talk on a phone. Oh yeah, *that* sounds normal. Of course this one would have to be in person. Kyle agreed to accompany me, but he suggested that we take along some muscle – just in case. So we rounded up Babs and Peg and set out for the gym.

[CHAPTER 23]

I was vaguely aware that women wrestled, but honestly, that fact never really penetrated my sphere of consciousness. If it had, I never would have set foot inside the building. I could tell by their reaction that at least two of my companions were having similar misgivings. There was nowhere safe to look or even stand for that matter. It was wall to wall creepy.

You just had the feeling that everyone and everything was watching you, and they thought YOU were the freak. Everything was dirty and sweaty and loud. Even the wall posters were violent and covered in the filth of god knows what. I could feel myself breaking into a cold sweat. I just wanted to leave – and pronto. As I was about to suggest a sudden departure we heard footsteps from across the floor.

"Yo, Kyle, long time." I guessed this was Cindy.

"Oh, um, hi there Cindy," responded Kyle.

Gulp. This chick was built like Paul Bunyan on steroids. Apparently steroids can be problematic to hair health as her mane of tacky bottle-blond spikes stuck out in varying lengths - in some cases as long as six inches. The eye makeup cannot be described other than to say that it was clearly shoveled on with a backhoe. She was one scary bitch. I wanted to go home.

I could see that Kyle was not really delighted to be back in her acquaintance. Perhaps he'd forgotten just how bad the up-close and personal experience could be – or perhaps it had gotten worse since he'd last seen her. Either way I could see that Kyle was backing up against the wall and appeared to be about to bolt. Frankly, I would have been a half step behind him.

Out of the corner of my eye I could see Babs and Peg. Peg resembled Kyle and looked about to run for it, but Babs appeared remarkably calm. After a protracted pause that increased my sweat level to about triple, I thought I heard Babs saying something. As I shifted focus over to concentrate, sure enough, it was Babs and she was in charge.

"So Cindy, I'm hopin' you'll be willing to give us some autographs when we're done talkin'." She gushed. "My kids just love you."

"Hell yeah, love my fans," Cindy proudly crowed.

Well how do you like that? Who would have thought that Babs would be our secret weapon. Amazingly, that was all it took. One small connection and we were golden. Well, tacky, cheesy, very cheap golden – but golden nonetheless. While the rest of us stood by in awe, we watched Babs lead our witness through a series of probing questions about Claire's table on the night of the murder.

Babs handled the queen of hurt like a true champ. She managed to find out how Cindy ended up at Claire's table and how she knew the victim and what she thought of the happenings during that dinner. It turned out that Cindy had known Clovis from an early jaunt on the wrestling circuit – oh Clovis I'll definitely have some fun with this – that ended in a few broken bones and significantly less cash than Clovis had hoped. Will wonders never cease?

Cindy was sure that Clovis was not the murderer because after the dinner she ran into Clovis in the bathroom and proceeded to tell her that she was an embarrassment to women everywhere. Cindy yelled, Clovis cried, Cindy yelled some more, Clovis hyperventilated and they agreed to part friends. Cindy walked Clovis to her car and saw her drive toward home – looking like something the cat would have dragged in. Everyone who knows Clovis would testify that she would never murder someone while looking like that!

I felt just the littlest bit sad for Clovis. Knowing this could certainly cut down on her ability to "be the brunt of the gossip." A prudent woman would be wise to lay low for a while under the circumstances. I was confident, however, that within no time Clovis would come up with a whole new reason for everyone to be talking about her. It was her greatest talent.

At this point it seemed like the right time to take our leave. We'd come, we'd conquered, in a manner of speaking, and we were ready to move on, I thought, but right about that time I heard something come out of Babs' mouth that caused my heart to skip a beat.

"Hey Cindy," goaded Babs, "how about seein' if one of us can kick your butt?"

I turned to look at the mild-mannered Babs that I thought I

knew – and there she stood grinning from ear to ear. Well Babs was planning on taking the video and Kyle certainly didn't qualify. That left... oh god! Before I had a chance to turn tail and run, I heard.

"Got an outfit that'll work on blondie there."

Aarrgghhhh!!! Blondie, that was me! I could hardly believe my ears and would have beat feet out the front door had not Peg and Babs grabbed my arms and jockeyed me into the dressing room. Before I knew it they had me all trussed up in a Golden Warrior leotard looking like a cheap hooker's aging Mama. It was so wrong. When they hauled me out to the ring I could see the look of horror on Kyle's face. I know he would have helped had he not been outnumbered by three determined and surprisingly strong women. All hope was lost.

I was tossed unceremoniously in the ring and turned to see the horrifying sight of Hog Jowl Cindy climbing in through the ropes. My life flashed before my eyes and my legs turned to rubber. Lucky for me Peg seemed to have some experience in managing fighters. Next thing I knew I was on my feet face to face with the terror of Omaha. If that weren't bad enough the eagle-eyed videographer, Babs, had a camera trained on us poised and ready for action. Please tell me this wasn't happening.

In reality I had very little to worry about. Cindy made short work of me. She tossed me around the ring for a few minutes like a spring salad, leaving me a little nauseous with a slightly bloody nose. From all accounts Babs got a video worth praising, and Cindy got a late afternoon workout. I was half led, half carried back to the dressing room for Peg to clean up and redress. It took Peg, Babs and

Kyle to carry me out to the car. No one said a word.

Back at the office I was able to climb out of the car on my own steam.

I said "Kyle."

"Don't Donna, we'll never speak of it," he answered.

I knew he meant it. But I also knew Babs had video.

[CHAPTER 24]

There have been many times when I've dreaded meeting Donny at the elevator – but none more than this. How had he found out so fast? No matter, life as I knew it was over. And the worst part – Donny never said a word. He just led me into the creative living room. By the time I got there the video was already playing to a packed house. Needless to say, my appearance in the room made quite a stir. As I turned to walk back toward my office a vile and horrible thing occurred – I caught a glimpse of myself in the ring with Cindy. In my worst nightmare several million times over I could not imagine looking more horrific than I did on that screen. At that moment I knew: even in death Claire had managed to best me. Well played, my worm-eaten, daisy-pushing foe, well played.

Home was calling me. I just wanted to get in bed and pull the covers up over my head. I walked into the front hallway from the garage door and sensed something odd almost immediately. I rushed in to the kitchen to find Jon at the computer with a pained yet puzzled expression on his face. He looked about halfway between crying and getting sick. Before I had a chance to say anything he uttered two little words to confirm my worst fears. YouTube.

[CHAPTER 25]

The next day was the first day of the rest of my life. Corny yes, but my only chance of survival. I called Kyle and asked him to meet me at Crane's coffee near the old Peony Park. I sat waiting for him in dark glasses and a hat. Yeah, maybe I was making too much of yesterday's debacle – but could I afford to take that chance?

Kyle walked in and expressed no surprise at my incognito appearance – he would have done the same in my place.

"How is it I never knew you worked with a psycho like that before?" I started.

"No, Donna, I swear she was not like that when we worked together," he countered. "I mean, she wasn't exactly cute and perky but I never would have expected this," Kyle admitted. "Seeing Cindy in her wrestling persona came as a total shock to me. You hear things but you can't really begin to imagine until you see it with your own eyes. I don't know how she went from being a slightly butch, extremely tailored business professional to mistress of the darkness. It kind of shakes your faith in everything you know. Guess I should have listened to all those snarky jokes a little more closely. Live and learn."

Time for philosophizing was over. We had to get back on track with our investigation. Hell, at this point I wouldn't have minded dropping the whole thing and getting back to normal. These past few days had been eventful, but it was the kind of excitement that shaves years off your life and ages you prematurely. I was starting to think maybe I was not cut out for the life of an investigator. A little boredom would be very welcome at this point. Unfortunately we'd committed to a course of action that seemed destined to follow us around until it reached its natural conclusion. At this point we were little more than pawns getting batted around by circumstances surrounding Claire's murder, and maybe we were in over our heads.

"Kyle what do you think really happened?" I blurted.

"You mean Claire's murder?" he asked thoughtfully. "I'm not sure I could hazard a guess at this point. I mean, it's frustrating and they say the more time that passes the colder the trail – but right now nothing seems clear to me. If I were forced to venture a guess though, I'd have to go with the whole bribery, threat, illegal thing she had going on through her work. That seems like the only thing important enough to commit a murder over."

"Good point," I countered. "But, don't they always say look to the simple solution, doesn't that whole thing seem incredibly convoluted to you?"

"Well sure, Donna, but the murderer didn't say, 'Oh, this is too complicated for me to commit a murder over,' you know?" Kyle reasoned.

He had a point. Of course the level of complexity was not responsible for causing the murder to occur. I was starting to think like a TV detective. and that would not help us get this thing solved. I had to start thinking about the people involved and which of them seemed unstable enough to do something this extreme. Odds were it wasn't an organized crime hit – someone got really emotional and she pushed them over the edge. Sounds exactly like Claire – but who could she have angered to that extent?

"You know, Kyle, I keep going back to the husband," I offered. "Usually real murders happen closest to home and family."

"I don't like Garth as a perp for this, Donna," Kyle rejoined.

"Don't LIKE him as a PERP, where did that come from, Kojak?" I goaded.

Kyle blushed. "Oh sorry, I was watching Psyche with my son last night. Guess I just picked up a few of those terms. I knew they sounded ridiculous after they were out of my mouth but I have to admit it felt pretty cool saying them," he admitted.

"No sweat, you're among friends, " I magnanimously replied. "Besides, it's not as though you haven't seen me in any somewhat compromising situations since this whole thing began," I finished, referencing my recent day of infamy.

"Oh wait a minute," Kyle started, "that could be it, compromising situations."

"Huh?"

"The girlfriend. I'd be willing to bet it wasn't Garth. But, I wouldn't be overly surprised to find it was the girlfriend – Lacy," Kyle gushed.

He had a point. It was the simplest solution in the universe. Woman scorned and woman who is responsible for scorn duke it out. It could be that second woman has more of a vested interest in making sure the guy is available for her future plans. Get rid of the nasty, shrewish, dare I say even fiendish wife and you've killed several large birds with one stone. That's an avenue we really needed to pursue.

"You know, Kyle, I definitely think you have something here," I offered. "But I keep going back to that forensic report. If we just knew the stature and strength of the murderer we might be able to eliminate certain suspects right off the bat. I'm not even giving up on the notion of Clovis as perp until I know the physical evidence wouldn't support her in a trial."

"Excellent point. Maybe when we get to the office we can push either Donny or Liv to focus on getting more details from the coroner's report," Kyle determined.

"Great idea. In fact, get them both on it. A little interim win would spur both teams on. You know like handing a piece of bloody meat over to the wolves – once they get a taste they'll kill for more."

"Geez, Donna you've really got to work on those analogies," Kyle choked. "They are brutal."

Well, you have to admit, I'm nothing if not colorful. But Kyle made a good point. I'd have to tone it down or risk breaking concentration for the sake of a stupid joke - easier said than done..

[CHAPTER 26]

Kyle and I decided that the best way to incentivize the teams would be to get them together for a joint recap meeting and rank order the information we felt would be most helpful in wrapping things up. All calendars were clear for a 10 a.m. meeting so we set it up in the Portfolio Room, our biggest and grandest conference room next to the theater we shared with JQH.

As I walked into the Portfolio Room at five minutes to ten and could see that everyone was present and accounted for, I glanced at my watch. Holy crap! This had to be a record for a Marcel internal meeting. These people were pumped! I guess it literally took a murder to get a meeting started on time - good thing I didn't say that out loud! Once I found a seat, Kyle began the meeting.

"Good morning everyone," he began. "Today we're going to review the leads that we've been working on and decide on our next steps."

It took about fifteen minutes for Kyle to review everything that we knew about Claire's murder. Then he took another ten or so to outline some of the most probable possibilities. As I watched the various facial reactions in the room while he worked his way through the data, I realized that as much as we already knew, there was much more that we didn't know. It was especially interesting watching Liv and Donny. Neither one of them had a poker face – although I'm sure they both thought they held their cards close to the vest. Hah! Not by a long shot!

I could see from Liv's reaction that she had a lot more dirt on Lacy, the girlfriend. Sadly for Liv, my keen powers of observation enabled me to see that Donny had also made that connection. Oh, there would definitely be some corporate espionage between camps. Luckily for Liv, it wasn't long before she got her turn. Donny's reaction to the mention of the coroner's report told me, and Liv, that he had something up his sleeve as well. Unfortunately, his reaction also made it fairly evident that he wasn't planning on sharing anytime soon. I couldn't blame him for keeping it under his shirt in a competition – but man, we could sure use some of that information to help keep things moving forward.

It occurred to me that it would be in our best interest to leave Donny to Kyle. I mean, let's face it, I'm about as subtle as a Rolls Royce in the Wal Mart parking lot, but Kyle, with his quiet and unassuming ways could usually get blood out of a stone without the stone ever being the wiser. I like that, I'm a Rolls and Donny's a stone. Yes, this was clearly a job for calm, cool and collected Kyle.

Next up was an animated but carefully guarded Q&A. If looks could kill Donny and Liv would have rubbed out half their team flashing their "no, no don't say anything about that" signals every time someone said a word. Come on guys, have a little faith in your teams! After that – meeting adjourned. We dispersed to finish the morning's duties and let the teams set their action plans. I could tell from some of the smug looks I saw going out the conference room door that almost everyone thought they had garnered more than they'd revealed. It should be a very interesting next few days to say the least.

With everyone else gone Kyle and I had a chance to 'post mortem' the meeting.

"I think that went well, don't you?" Kyle began.

"No complaints," I replied. "Well, maybe one or two. Kyle, we have to get that forensic information from Donny and we've got to crack Liv for the girlfriend skinny."

"I know, I saw that too. Subtle they're not," Kyle mused.

Man, that was the closest thing to a shot I'd ever heard from Kyle. I have to admit to feeling a bit shocked, but in a good way. He was still light years away from the obnoxious smart asses that comprised the vast majority of Marcel – the whole advertising industry in fact.

It seemed as though Kyle had all the heavy lifting to do. Maybe I would focus on actual agency work and let him run with the ball for a while. I could use a break anyway. Once we established that Kyle was the logical person to interrogate our two team captains we were ready to head back to our offices.

As I walked down the hall I stopped to talk to Billy and Reinhart. I waved to Camy and Janie. It had only been a few days since we'd begun our investigation, yet it seemed like a lifetime. I felt as though

I'd been neglecting the majority of the staff who'd been diligently at work while a handful of us had embarked on our not exactly excellent adventure. It felt good to be sort of back to normal. By the time I reached my office I was really starting to feel back in the old routine again. As I approached my desk, even the piles of untouched paperwork did not stifle my rising spirits. It all felt familiar and right now familiar was good.

I sat down and savored the moment, remembering a time when my most pressing concern was answering my phone calls and e-mails in a timely manner. E-mail seemed like the best place to get started, so I logged in and waited for my account to update. As usual, I scanned the overwhelming influx of e-mails for anything urgent or unusual. Nothing urgent – but there was an odd subject from earlier that morning. "Delete at your own risk." That was new. I thought I'd seen all the pushy sales gimmicks out there. The temptation to call their bluff was driving me – but curiosity won out. I opened the e-mail to see a brief but poignant message, "Snoops die." Oh shit. All of the anxiety connected with the investigation came rushing back. I felt foolish but my pulse was racing and my breathing quickened.

Okay be practical. Who sent it? I really couldn't make it out but I knew our IT guy would be able to track down the culprit. Oh, and I should probably give Warren a call. We were overdue checking in with her anyway. I left a message for Warren and ran to find Mark, our IT guy. I didn't want to keep that e-mail one second more than I had to.

After a few minutes of checking and digging, Mark sat back in my chair.

"It's the damndest thing," he mused. "I can't tell where the hell this is coming from. Somewhere in Omaha – I'm pretty sure of that, but I should be able to drill right in on the origin of this thing. It's been set up to make that virtually impossible. I think I'm going to go grab Lake and ask if he's ever seen anything like this before."

That didn't help my nerves at all, and there it was still staring defiantly at me. Imagine being beaten down by a one-sentence, just a fragment really – e-mail. I hated that more than I could say. Oh well, at least the appearance of the e-mail was starting to make me angry. I'd rather be angry than timid any day of the week. The killer was clearly calling me out and it was GO time! Okay you SOB, if that's what you want you've got yourself a battle. I headed over to Donny's office. One thing was for sure, I wanted the police to know every step this killer took – especially in relation to me! I would get Donny to fill his buddies in while I was waiting for Warren to call back. At times like these keeping busy, even if it's seemingly inconsequential, can keep you out of the loony bin!

To my great relief and surprise Donny was clearly extremely concerned at hearing the news of this latest e-mail. Most of us knew that Donny really cared more than he'd ever let on, but his gruff and callous persona could start to make you think that he really did believe you were the village idiot. I envisioned undergoing a lengthy period of assault and abuse after which I half expected Donny to reveal with a villainous laugh that he had solved the murder in order to pay the killer to terrorize and kill me. I know, I know, a bit melodramatic on my part – but Donny's barbs can start to make you think that way.

Instead I was greeted with outright gravity and deep concern. It was positively touching. And if that wasn't enough, after vowing to share the news with his buddies he personally vowed that no little pissant killer was going to touch a hair on my head. Now I was starting to choke up. He cared – Donny really cared. But to avoid getting altogether too gooey, I had to tell him to grow a pair and stop being so dorky. He immediately snapped back into Donny mode – but I'd always have "no little pissant!"

[CHAPTER 27]

Re-energized from my newly motivated anger, and feeling
significantly less vulnerable with Donny's vow to ensure my safety,
I was ready to do battle. But where to start? I had to wait for
Kyle to complete his handiwork in order to obtain most of the key
information. Anxious to get moving I grabbed a diet orange Sunkist
and started to review all of our most likely suspects. There was one
obvious angle that we hadn't even touched on. The angry insurance
man.

I recalled some of the speculation regarding that unlikely
scenario. Why would Claire have an inordinate number of dealings
with the insurance man for the outdoor company where she worked?
And why would the insurance man be openly angry in some of
those more recent conversations? It was definitely something that
warranted exploration. It seemed to be the one unaddressed area at
this point. But where to start? This called for another diet Sunkist,
but I had to be careful not to overdo that – nothing fun about a fake
sugar high.

It was the second diet Sunkist that kicked me into gear. I knew a salesperson who had worked at Toto just as Claire was starting out there. Tina liked Claire slightly less than I did. Let's face it – Claire was a fast worker. She could alienate virtually anyone with an hour to spare before lunch. It was a gift.

So Tina would probably be the most likely person to have the skinny on all the weird happenings at Toto. How did I not think of Tina before? Menopause? I made a mental note to kick myself for that thought. I really hate it when any lapse of memory in a woman anywhere from 43 through 65 is attributed to menopause. We forget things when we're 21 too! That kind of stereotyping we don't need!

Now, about Tina. I checked my contacts and couldn't find a recent number for her. It took me about a minute to Google her and get all the pertinent information. I called Tina and after a few minutes of catch-up we agreed to meet at Dante Pizzeria for a late lunch. That seemed like the most harmless and productive activity that I could muster while vigilantly maintaining my own safety. I would go from our secure parking garage at the office to the very public parking at the Legacy shops. From my vantage point at Dante I could watch my car at all times from a very public and very crowded sanctuary. Short of a drive-by shooting to or from lunch I couldn't imagine being any safer.

It really was good to see Tina and catch up. For the first half of our lunch we were just two colleagues relaxing and enjoying a leisurely visit. We even treated ourselves to a glass of white wine with our Cobb salads. It would be so nice to forget the whole mess even for just a brief respite. Height-wise, Tina was a little bit of a thing, but she was sporting an extra 30 – 35 pounds. Behind her back she garnered the ill conceived nickname of, what else, Tiny Tina – ouch. But, to give her credit, Tina's couture was more chic and elegant than anyone else in the market. Her hair style, nails and makeup were consistently flawless. The entire package that was Tina could make any woman, regardless of shape or stature, wish only to be thought of as nearly as good. She was an impressive force. It could have been why Claire hated her so much, but then did Claire ever really need a reason?

After a thoroughly decadent but bordering-on-healthy lunch it was time for getting down to business. Tina spent a good 30 minutes filling me in on fact and speculation as it related to Claire's tenure at Toto.

I had to laugh. Even with a new start, our victim could not help but engender animosity and downright hostility from virtually everyone in her path. She did, however, isolate the occasional lackey for her personal convenience and self aggrandizement: someone not quite bright enough to see through her incredibly obvious maneuverings, and who was dense enough to do her bidding without question. These were the poor lost souls who were left floundering by the wayside wondering what hit them when her dastardly dealings inevitably required that she move on.

Tina's revelations followed the typical Claire path of devastation as she wrought havoc on the formerly peaceful world of Toto. I had to shake my head, but I couldn't say I was surprised. Actually, Tina's commentary made me mindful of the one thing that never ceased to amuse me. Claire had never wanted to leave Marcel but she'd brought about her own downfall by making one fatally serious miscalculation. She thought Donny would be her lackey.

That seems inconsistent with her former m.o. She usually picked out an acknowledged dullard, never considering anyone as openly intelligent as Donny, but it really just proved to be an extension of her own arrogance and overblown self assurance. She thought next to her anyone was a dullard. The real catch was that she had actually reached the point where her gargantuan ego assumed that her far superior intellect would enable her to out-think and maneuver even someone as intelligent as Donny, and she completely discounted the old adage about playing with fire. It became her Kilimanjaro to conquer the superior intellect and make it her bitch. Through the whole thing Donny had known what she was thinking, and he let her.

Claire's end at Marcel came out of nowhere, much like the sound and the fury signifying nothing. She backed herself into a political corner – with a little help from us dullards – and had no choice but to cut her losses and move on. It was a glorious day!

I came out of my reverie and realized that I'd have to ask Tina to back up a few steps. I apologized and promised to pay closer attention. Tina was happy to comply. She knew the past few days had been pretty bizarre and didn't seem surprised that I was having some trouble getting focused and she was just as anxious to pick my brain about the circumstances surrounding the murder.

By now Tina's narrative had moved on to the entrance of the mysterious insurance guy, Kurt Vandemoore or Vandam as Claire liked to call him. She had some weird-ass nicknames for everyone, usually based on a twisted version of their last name, that were oddly contagious. She called me League, refusing to acknowledge that the "g" in my name was silent. Vandam had dated Claire when he was working at Fowler Mutual before her tenure at Marcel and her marriage to Garth. They were an unlikely pair just from a physical standpoint, she being the size of an average pro linebacker and he being a tiny little lump of a man with the pudgiest little chipmunk cheeks. She had been the one who helped him study for all of his level exams. Shortly after their breakup he'd been tossed out of the company unceremoniously for some nefarious dealings with vendors. Clearly they'd kept in touch. Most recently Vandam had started his own insurance agency but had been having trouble finding insurance companies that would be willing to let him represent them and sell their policies. His reputation had begun to precede him and things were getting tight.

Initially, the folks at Toto thought that Claire and Vandam might be having a little extramarital fling – a rekindling of the old flame if you will - the thought of which brought a slight gag reflex to both Tina and me. They seemed to spend an inordinate amount of time together. After a month or so at Toto, Tina continued, Claire began working on Collin. Collin Berry was the owner at Toto and the poor unfortunate who hired Claire away from Marcel. She wanted him to switch insurance carriers for his out-of-home company and work with Vandam.

It just so happened that Collin was in the market for a new carrier. The previous year he'd had a mishap with a worker trying to install a vinyl outdoor bulletin. As in many cases the winds were too strong and the vinyl bullwhipped in the installer's direction, knocking him off of a thirty foot platform to his death. Collin's insurance company at the time did not come through as he had hoped. So, it didn't really take long for Claire's constant badgering and manipulative counseling to take hold, especially since Collin thought of her as an insurance expert anyway - she never lost an opportunity to brag about her extensive insurance knowledge. She could certainly talk the talk. At that point, poor Collin was actually beginning to think that landing Claire had really begun to pay off – even though the stirrings of unrest among the natives at Toto had already begun to reach even his ears.

"But Tina," I couldn't wait to satisfy my curiosity, "what was all that rumor business about Claire and rezoning?"

"Hang on, I'm getting to that," Tina urged.

She went on to explain that in addition to pushing for a new insurance vendor, Claire had been pressing Collin relentlessly to make her a full partner and co-owner of Toto.

"So did he?" I was more than anxious for this pivotal piece of information.

Sensing my impatience, Tina did what any good storyteller would do to heighten the suspense. She went to the ladies' room. Man, did she take forever. Why was she taking so long? Did she have a pair of Depends on under that haute couture suit? Okay Donna, that was going way too far. Just relax and try to enjoy Tina's colorful and entertaining monologue. Too much of life is rushed unceremoniously. Besides, I knew the more I pushed the more Tina would make me work for it. Better to just leave the driving to Tina –

we'd get there eventually. Determined to shut up and let Tina tell her tale, I did what any good listener would do and waved the waitress over to order another round of white wine. What the hell – it would make "the ride" more fun!

With Tina back from the loo, we were starting to get down to brass tacks. Collin had actually called her to discuss the merits of making Claire a partner. Little did I realize then that Tina was about to drop a major bombshell on me. It seems she and Collin were an item so I really had hit the jackpot of sources. Hallelujah! Of course we had to take a moment to discuss all the particulars related to this juicy new piece of news. I toasted the couple with my new glass of white wine and we jumped back into our main topic – Claire. Tina stated with finality that Collin had never had any real intention of making Claire a partner. Unbeknownst to Claire, it was Tina who was getting ready to partner up with Collin. And Claire was none too happy when she accidentally stumbled upon that little piece of information.

It all made perfect sense now. Tina had left Toto for two reasons, to keep their relationship under wraps a bit longer and to join up with the transit company that Collin had hoped to purchase to round out his offerings in the market. That made perfect sense, at least until Claire came into the picture. As usual, Claire's agenda was thinly disguised as a means of helping Toto, but far more clearly a means of helping Claire in her personal advancement.

At first, Claire demonstrated that she really wanted to be co-owner of Toto. She even invested a great deal of time and energy into evaluating zoning issues that made growth in the market somewhat challenging. In joining Toto, Claire had learned from Collin that the biggest single obstacle to the growth of his business was the fact that many of the prime potential out-of-home locations were made impossible due to antiquated zoning laws. If these laws could be refined to give Collin more freedom to build, especially west of 90th Street, there was no end to the success he would realize. But zoning laws are notoriously difficult to change. The old guard of the city oversees the zoning commission to ensure that Omaha doesn't become another Las Vegas with bright and garish ornamentation overshadowing the natural beauty inherent to the area. To change these laws could take nothing short of an act of God!

In her usual delusion of overconfidence, Claire was convinced that if she could find a way to change the zoning in his favor, Collin would be convinced that she was so valuable he'd want her as a partner and would overlook her inability and/or unwillingness to make any financial investment in the company. History does tend to repeat itself and Claire was exhibiting a definite pattern of behavior here.

Tina chuckled at the recollection. Without a financial investment there was no possibility of an ownership position in Toto – even for a fiancée. Claire's business acumen proved tragically naïve, once again. Tina went on to explain that by the time Collin realized why Claire's interest in zoning had suddenly become so intense, he had also begun to realize that her mere existence was causing everyone on his staff to contemplate jumping ship. At that point he began to consider moving her out with a minimum of disruption. That's just about the time when Claire's newly fueled frustration shifted her focus from building to destroying.

Apparently Claire had had Vandam in her hip pocket in the event that all of the plotting did not ultimately meet her unrealistic expectations. It had just started to appear as though her hard work on the zoning commission might pay off – but any payoff, she was beginning to understand, would undoubtedly still take years to materialize. On top of that, Claire had been unable to seal the ownership deal with Collin. Frankly, once her ownership position appeared moot her thoughts turned to one thing: how can I profit handsomely from this whole experience? You've got to give her credit. At least she learned one thing in her years of selfish and destructive plotting – have a Plan B, and Plan B was the easily influenced Vandam.

According to Tina, Collin had filled her in on Claire's Plan B – in spades. Apparently, Claire had unearthed some very old and decidedly unusable bulletins, those 14′ x 48′ monster signs typically seen on the side of a major roadway, bought by Collin in his purchase of Toto. These were bulletins in areas that were currently low traffic and in dire need of a fair amount of maintenance in order to be saleable to any client. Collin had not yet decided how to proceed with them since he wasn't convinced that any revenue generated on these inferior older boards would compensate for the cost of bringing them up to current standard. Even if they were updated, that still wouldn't rectify the location problems. He would gladly have sold them had he thought anyone would be interested in purchasing. These properties had been sitting around for a year or two just waiting for Collin to formulate an action plan. After a great deal of snooping, Claire had unearthed all of these locations. Realizing that they would not have Collin's attention, at least for a while yet, she concocted her plan around them.

Under a false corporate Toto identity, Claire purchased an inordinate amount of insurance from Vandam for each of these locations. Her intention, it seems, was to destroy each of the bulletin structures and collect on the extraordinarily high insurance policy before Collin suspected anything. Claire and Vandam had already agreed to share in the windfall – as Vandam had had to do some finagling in order to get the policies through.

Unfortunately for the greedy pair, Collin stumbled upon an aberration in a routine check of his paperwork which ultimately led him to their duplicitous scheme. Once he reconstructed their plan and realized its implications, Collin confronted Claire leading to a knockdown drag-out battle. Claire knew that the jig was up. Collin, being an incredibly fair man, offered to let Claire search for another position before leaving Toto. Who else would do that under the circumstances?

All of the pieces were finally starting to fall into place for me. Claire had sure been busy since leaving Marcel, it was nothing short of incredible. When she couldn't own an ad agency without making any financial investment she went on to the world of outdoor. She never learned that you can't get something for nothing, even if you're extraordinary – and she was far from that!

Tina finished her monologue by adding that Claire had been in a flat-out panic over the past few weeks. She had started to realize that between burning as many bridges as she had and the fact that the economy had reduced the overall number of positions in the market, it was going to be a long uphill battle to find herself a comparable position. In fact, that realization had prompted another major battle between Claire and Collin. She was desperate and lashing out indiscriminately.

I felt for Tina. She'd been through quite a bit on Collin's behalf. But, I couldn't help wondering how problematic Claire had become for Collin, or for Vandam for that matter. Could either – could any of them have literally had more than they could take? I hated to suspect Tina after she'd been so open and informative about all the dark and dirty secrets that had Claire on the ropes. I was really hoping that the coroner's report would rule out anyone of diminutive stature. That would clear Tina and would help get Clovis off our backs – until she found a new angle to torture us with.

Tina and I said our good-byes and she kindly suggested that I look for a wedding invitation in the mail. I really didn't expect to be invited to Tina and Collin's wedding but what the hell – murder made strange bedfellows.

[CHAPTER 28]

Back at the office I made a beeline for Kyle. Yes, he was there and ready to share. After I briefed him on my lunch with Tina he remarked somewhat sheepishly "Well Donna, I was the one with the key assignment and it looks as though you scooped me big time."

"Don't be modest, Kyle," I admonished impatiently. "What've you got?"

"Well," he began, "I started with Liv, and you know her. She's not into hidden agendas and secrets – not even for the sake of a "stupid competition." I believe those were her exact words. But Liv certainly did know something about the other woman, Lacy. "

It took Kyle about 10 minutes to fill me in on the Lacy scoop. Apparently Liv served on a charitable board with Lacy's mother. As much as Liv did not want to hear TMI, she failed to duck out fast enough after the last board meeting and was cornered by Lacy's distraught mom, Olivia. Olivia was pretty upset about the whole murder/affair thing. She was looking for someone on whom she could unburden herself, and that lucky person was Liv. They stopped at Urban Wine for a glass of wine and some munchies and Liv got quite an earful.

Apparently Olivia was really torn. Prior to the murder, Garth and Lacy had come to her and declared their undying love for each other. Garth wanted to be kind to Claire – the sensitivity had not been lost on Olivia – and would marry Lacy as soon as he could humanely extricate himself from his current situation. Once Claire was murdered, Olivia had been unable to shake the fear that her now very soon to be new son-in-law might possibly have murdered his current wife to make room for his intended new one. Her gut told her that Garth could not be a killer – but she knew that many wife killers were good old boys next door, at least that's what every one of their neighbors ever interviewed on TV has ever said, until conclusive evidence put them on death row. Olivia was a wreck.

"But what about Lacy, did Liv know what was on Lacy's mind?" I pushed eagerly.

"Good segue, Donna, I was just getting to that," Kyle assured me.

He went on to detail Olivia's concerns over Lacy's blind faith in Garth. In fact, Lacy was pushing to get Claire and Garth's son back from his temporary residence with Claire's parents so the three of them could set up housekeeping and start living together as a family. At least Garth was smart enough to realize that it was way too soon for that kind of upheaval. He thought his son could use a little grandma nurturing at a tragic time like this, and that his in-laws needed some kind of mission to help keep them from falling apart completely. Even solid Nebraska farm stock like Claire's parents could hardly withstand a tragic blow like this and continue moving forward with everything as usual. She observed that Garth was being the model father and son-in-law by sleeping on his in-laws' couch every night. It's pretty clear that his main concern was for the welfare of his boy and secondarily he wanted to support the boy's grandparents.

"Interesting, Kyle. Garth and Lacy were farther along in their relationship than I'd realized, " I mused. "This was not just some shoddy affair – they planned a future together. Was there any evidence as to how much of this was known to Claire?"

"Actually, yes," he replied. "Olivia said that, according to Lacy, Claire and Garth had practically been separated when the two had started their relationship. Garth never held anything back from Claire – there were no dirty little secrets. Garth even had the impression – although it had never been confirmed – that Claire had started up with her old boyfriend, Kurt. So it all sounds above board and pretty consistent with Tina's version from lunch."

"Hmmph," I countered. "Doesn't sound like anything worth killing over does it – or is that the obvious thing that the "other woman" tells her mother – I just don't know?"

"Well, there may be a bit more to it," Kyle cautioned. "Recently, Claire had intimated that it might be in her best interest to relocate to a new market."

That made perfect sense if she'd burned all her bridges in this market, and lord knows at the rate she was burning bridges, it was a wonder she could fit in full-time work. It's totally consistent with Tina's impression that Claire knew full well that her days in the market were numbered – she had burned her last bridge here!

Kyle continued, "Garth and Lacy were well ensconced in this market and had no interest in moving anywhere. Garth was anything but pleased at the prospect of being separated from his son. I gather they were starting to have some extremely heated discussions about the boy."

"Ahhh, the plot thickens," I offered in my best Holmesian impression. "Garth makes it back onto the suspect list – and Lacy with her blind support of Garth."

"Well…"started Kyle.

Before Kyle had a chance to finish his update on Lacy and Garth, Donny poked his head in to share some news.

"Hey Donna," he gushed, "just talked to my cop pals and they've figured out where your threatening e-mail originated. "

I waited with baited breath.

"From the university," Donny concluded.

"What does that mean?" I countered.

"Well, it doesn't give them as much to go on as they'd hoped 'cause a lot of people have access to those computers," Donny offered. "But, it does move their staff and administration higher up on the list of suspects. Even students are getting a second, harder look."

"Yeah, or the killer knew that would happen and chose to use one of those computers for just that reason," I speculated dejectedly.

"True enough," Donny agreed. "But, it does make sense to take extra precautions when dealing with anyone from campus. And with any luck the police will narrow the pool down further. Sorry I don't have anything more definitive – I'll let you know when I do."

"Hey Donny, I really appreciate your help on this," I assured him. "I don't mean to seem ungrateful, I'm just scared and I'm feeling a bit like a prisoner myself."

Both Donny and Kyle were quick to assure me that they would do everything in their power to make me feel safe. It meant a lot but I still felt very much like a victim – and I hated it.

After Donny left, Kyle started filling me in on their somewhat frustrating conversation from earlier in the day. Kyle's account of Donny's determined attempt to reveal nothing – and his ultimate inability to keep from bragging about what he'd learned served to cheer me up considerably. After listening to the entire account, I congratulated Kyle for his masterful manipulation of Donny. Kyle said he wasn't very proud of it, but I could tell that secretly he was pleased with himself. Donny was a tough nut to crack and Kyle had broken through his shell like a hot knife through butter. I wasn't sure if I was more excited about the information he got or the fact that he'd successfully wrangled it out of the master! I also knew that, once this info became public, Donny would claim that he had deliberately leaked it to Kyle. He's just so predictable!

In a nutshell, Donny had told Kyle he'd been able to get several new pieces of information from the coroner's report through his cop friends. He intimated that it wasn't everything, but Kyle did not have a strong feeling that Donny, or even his cop friends, knew any more than had been revealed.

What they did learn was that Claire was killed by someone about her height of 6'2", which ruled out Clovis, Tina and virtually every woman who'd been a suspect. Clovis would be devastated. The coroner's report also revealed that the perpetrator had weighed somewhere between 220 and 250 pounds. The weight discrepancy came from the continued inability to pinpoint the murder weapon – but apparently they had some ideas that had not yet come forth. The report also indicated that Claire had been struck from behind and had most likely been unaware of being followed at all. There was no evidence of a struggle and the blow suggested that she had not even turned around to face her assailant. Indications were that the first blow rendered her unconscious if not completely brain dead. The two additional blows were most likely gratuitous. This was starting to get interesting.

Kyle and I took a minute to feel comforted by the news. If the coroner's report was accurate Claire had not been fearful nor had she suffered any pain. No matter how awful she was in life, we could not wish pain and suffering on her in her final moments. We were happy for her and for her family. Yeah, maybe we were softies, and had the shoe been on the other foot, a thought that had crossed my mind in occasional moments of panic, it's possible that she might have wished us maximum pain and suffering – but we just weren't capable of that kind of cruelty.

[CHAPTER 29]

By the time I got back to my desk I had messages from Liv, Shell
and Mel. All of the witnesses had been interviewed and nothing new
had been determined. Time to let Clovis know that not only did she
check out with witnesses, when I say "check out" I'm just talking in
terms of being a suspect, which is totally independent of the obvious
certifiable lunatic factor we all know is her constant state, but that
forensics had also ruled her out as a suspect. The thought of calling
and spending the next hour on the phone with Clovis was too painful
to contemplate. Then it dawned on me – I'd just send her a message
through Facebook. I know, I know, but I would totally defriend her
after the investigation. I swear!

In retrospect it was probably my best alternative, but when I first
opened her Facebook page I began to have second thoughts. A quick
glance told me to hit the message link and get out of her business
ASAP, but as with a devastating train wreck the temptation to look
proved too great. After five minutes of reading comments from
Clovis and her friends regarding her on again/off again relationship

status with Bat, my head was reeling and I was starting to feel mildly nauseous. Déjà vu took me back to a time in junior high where it felt as though life would never be anything but extreme emotion and torture. As the pain mounted, I very nearly exited her Facebook page entirely but a brief realization that to back out now would mean a one-on-one phone call brought me back to reality. I clicked the link and composed my message to Clovis. I kept it short but sweet. "No one thinks you did it. Forensics has proven that you didn't. Happy to help. Congrats!" I exited Facebook so fast I'm sure I set a record.

I had done my good deed for the day. In spades!

At this point I took a few deep breaths and pulled out my notes on the murder. I reviewed them methodically, correcting every reference that the new forensic and anecdotal information had recanted. Damn, today's information really changed a lot of what we thought we'd known and/or suspected, but were we any closer to finding resolution? It occurred to me that being an amateur detective was a lot like attempting a jigsaw puzzle where a quarter of the pieces had been destroyed. There was no way we were going to uncover every piece of evidence and get at the whole truth, and that would always bug me. Even if the murderer were found and brought to justice, what was really driving me was solving the puzzle and fitting all the pieces into place, and there was not much chance of that. There was just no way of knowing if there would ever be enough puzzle pieces to come up with any kind of a firm conclusion.

I made a few phone calls and got caught up with the work on my desk and in my e-mail, but something was bothering me. I tried to convince myself that our progress today was a reason to feel good about things, but that nagging, unsettled feeling continued. Something about that threatening e-mail – and not just the fact that I was definitely starting to feel real fear – there was more to it. Try as I might I couldn't get my subconscious to focus long enough to do any real good. Maybe my four o'clock brainstorming meeting would help to clear my brain and I would have more luck later. It doesn't hurt to hope.

Shell ran the brainstorming meeting and it adjourned at 5:40. My brain definitely felt more clear – in fact it felt downright empty, and that felt pretty good for a change. Time to call it a night. I'd go home, grab a glass of Kim Crawford and relax in the hot tub for a bit. Man, that sounded good. At times like these I was glad to live only three miles from the office. I headed down to the parking garage in anticipation of an evening of decadent relaxation, but something made the hairs on the back of my neck stand at attention. I tried to tell myself that I was just being overly anxious due to recent events. I would get in my car in the private parking garage and drive the three miles to my house and the comfort of my own garage where Jon and the bulldogs awaited my return. Safe, simple and just what I needed.

I pulled out of the parking garage which I normally considered a huge luxury for owners and partners. Tonight it's deserted stark cement décor made it seem eerily quiet and tomblike. As my car cleared the large metal door, the lights of a large black SUV parked just outside snapped on. Oh well, so what? And so what that the same big honking vehicle began to pull out behind me. I got to the end of our parking lot and pulled out into the service road with the SUV still in tow. There were those hairs on the back of my neck again

– damn – they felt as though I'd sprayed them with hairspray. As I pulled onto 144th Street I was still being followed by the SUV – odd. Then, I swung my car onto the Dodge entrance ramp – the SUV still on my tail.

At this point my hands were sweating and I was feeling rather annoyed with myself. "How many times does this very thing happen and you never notice it," I thought. "Stop looking for trouble!"

When the SUV followed me onto the off ramp for 156th Street I was in full-out panic. Not wanting to lead the murderer straight into my garage, I was frantic for what to do and where to go. I wanted to call Jon but feared that my hands were shaking too much to use my Blue Tooth. I had to think fast. I'd get back on Dodge heading east and see if the SUV stayed behind me. To my great dismay not only did the SUV maintain its vigilant pursuit, it started moving closer and appeared to be gearing up to ram into me.

Now I was sweating bullets. I started praying out loud and could feel the odd teardrop make its way down my cheek. Where could I go to escape this fate? I didn't want to end like Claire!! With both hands on the wheel I decided to try to lose my pursuer. I started weaving in and out of traffic to no avail – the SUV driver was as determined as I. Then it dawned on me. If I could make it to a popular restaurant there'd be too many witnesses, and maybe I could make a break for it and run inside. I set my sights for Bonefish in the Regency Court mall, and I put the pedal to the metal. Between weaving and speeding I made it to the refuge of Regency before the SUV. I pulled up right outside and jumped out of the still running car ready to bolt for the front door. Just as I reached the restaurant's door pull and certain safety, I heard a familiar and unbelievably annoying voice call to me.

"Donna?" Clovis entreated me, "For god's sake what's your rush?"

Are you freakin' kidding me? It was Clovis in the SUV? At that moment the thought of killing her and spending the rest of my life behind bars seemed like the only logical course of action. It would be soooo worth it!

"Clovis?" I screamed with an anger that surprised even me. "Just what in the hell mofo@#$$@%%& did you think you were doing?" I demanded.

Before she could answer I hopped back into my car and moved it to a proper parking spot. Then I got out to commit murder.

"Now Donna, before you go and get all PMSy about things," she said in her best "I'm sure I can calm you down" voice.

PM What? Oh god this woman really did not want to live. I was speechless, and that never happens. I'm guessing my face was a regular carnival of colors and expressions ranging from murderous to deeply pained and back again. I know when I get like this it usually serves to clear the area. People behave as though someone has just released the Kracken – and someone had.

As she watched my facial contortions it finally dawned on Clovis that she could potentially be in line for some grave bodily harm. In a rush of panic she grabbed her cell and called Kyle.

"Kyle, you'd better get here right away, something has happened to Donna and I'm really not sure what to do," I heard her say.

God bless Kyle. Before I regained the ability to speak I saw his lovely SUV pull into the parking lot. He must have set a land speed record in getting here. He parked and ran over to me in time for my croaked, "Get her out of my sight."

That's all I had to say. Kyle cajoled and coaxed until he got Clovis in her vehicle and on her way. Don't get me wrong, it took him a few minutes – but he realized that there was a lot riding on getting her the hell out of there.

Once she was gone, Kyle came back over to check on my recovery.

"Donna, I think you could use a nice glass of white wine right about now. How about going into Bonefish as long as we're right here?" Kyle offered realizing that I was not in the best shape to drive home.

"Thanks Kyle," I replied very sincerely, "but I really want to be home and I know you promised your wife that you'd take her out for a nice dinner this evening. I'm not about to ruin that for either of you, but you're very sweet,"

"Donna, you know Lori loves you, and she would kill me if she thought I rushed home when you were in need of some consoling. Lori is the most understanding wife there is and she would totally prefer to have me stay with you until you feel ready to drive yourself. Besides, I know Jon would do the same for me if the situations were in reverse," Kyle pleaded.

"Really Kyle, I'll be fine. But I will fill you in on what's going on here," I asserted.

Once I'd filled Kyle in on our hell ride through West Omaha I thought it was I who would have to buy him a glass of white wine.

I don't ever remember seeing Kyle so angry. He even murmured something about strangling her while he had the chance. Poor Kyle had been so concerned about my becoming fearful over today's activities and suddenly, out of nowhere, came "little miss no one else matters but me" to put the ever lovin' fear of God into me. He was livid.

I have to admit, seeing Kyle come to my defense really helped to calm me down over the whole ridiculous incident. As logic began to seep back where pure animal emotion had recently resided, my main thought was, "We know she's certifiable, so why does it always catch us by surprise?"

I thanked Kyle profusely – had he not been there there's no telling what might have happened to dear little Clovis, and I really wasn't serious about being willing to spend life in prison for the satisfaction of being the one to end that tortured little existence. Once we were satisfied that we were both functioning and logical, we said our good-byes and drove home to our respective spouses. I felt very fortunate to have a friend like Kyle.

[CHAPTER 30]

The next morning, word of my mishap was all over the agency. I was a little surprised at first. Kyle was not one to spread information of any kind. He understood the value of keeping some things private. Within minutes I learned that Kyle had not been the purveyor of this news. It had been documented on Clovis' Facebook page. Apparently along with some candid shots that she'd surreptitiously snapped. And if that wasn't enough she was Tweeting about it on the hour!

"Man, Donna, I don't think I've ever seen you that mad." This from Boneman – our graphic genius. "That killer dude better watch his package."

Great, it wasn't bad enough being a menopausal Neanderthal in front of the best, youngest and brightest in the business, I was also going to be labeled as the scary killer-maimer to boot. We were getting today off to a really good start! Thanks, Clovis.

Amazingly, in her portrayal of my escapade there was another driver taunting me on the road and Clovis just happened to be there

166

to lend a helping hand. In her defense I have to say that she made me out to be one tough Mama. I guess that was my payback should I choose to go with her version. Ah hell, at this point my legend preceded me. Who was I to disappoint all my eager supporters. Funny, Clovis had said she was a good publicist but we'd never seen any evidence of that – until now.

I was being assailed from every angle. The whole staff was eager to show their wholehearted support and I have to admit it was incredibly heartwarming. That is until you came back to the reality that the whole dire episode was brought about by Clovis' refusal to acknowledge that she might not be a key player in this murder after all. Oh yeah, did I mention that's why she tried to run me off the road? She needed verbal confirmation of my Facebook message to truly believe that she was not the prime suspect. The scariest part of this whole thing was that you'd think she'd know that – whatever the police might think – she WASN'T the killer. Is it possible she'd actually forgotten that kind of important fact?

I touched base with Kyle to see how he was faring this morning. That's when he filled me in on what had really happened the night before. Clovis had read my Facebook message and she'd freaked out. She'd jump into her black rental SUV to try and catch me on my way home. The coroner's report must be wrong, she'd rationalized to Kyle. Was it possible she would no longer be the center of this whole investigation? She wasn't prepared for that eventuality. She needed more, and let me tell you – last night she came damn close to getting more. For the life of me I can't imagine a way of getting more attention other than to be the actual murder victim. Sure you'd have to be dead – small price to pay for that kind of attention in Clovis' world. Please, God get me away from Clovis before I really started understanding some of the things she was saying.

After our brief morning homage to Clovis – this was becoming something of a habit, a bad habit -- Kyle and I turned our thoughts to, well honestly, any part of the murder investigation that did not involve Clovis. We just needed a break. One thing that suddenly dawned on both of us was that the killer was clearly focused on my involvement in the investigation. I mean others – actually a boatload of others – were involved in the hunt for Claire's vicious killer – so why was I the only one who appeared to be receiving those threatening notes? Kyle was the one to actually come up with the somewhat chilling conclusion.

"Donna," he uttered in a faltering voice, "in order to find the killer we have to take a closer look at you and your interactions with people. Somehow there's a link to you."

***

Gulp.

He was right. I hadn't seen it that way before, but who would send threatening messages aside from the killer? And why would they single me out unless they had a somewhat unrealistic view of me as the master detective? As scary as that was it made a lot of sense.

We decided to run our theory by Donny and Liv. They concurred. And they took a moment from their heated competition to suggest – jointly – that the police be advised that this might just be the angle that would pay off for them in the end. We were looking for a twisted individual who knew me and was intimidated by reports of my murder-solving prowess.

Kyle put in a call to Detective Warren and she agreed to swing by Marcel on her way to the coroner's. After briefing her on our theory, she had to admit that it was an interesting and possibly worthwhile approach. So I was assigned a task force. There were detectives who would investigate me and everything I thought and everything I did. Other detectives would investigate everyone who knew me and had connections to Claire. And a third set of uniformed officers was assigned to guard me around the clock in case the killer tried to get near me again. All in all, my life would be relegated to the whims and actions of a group of six previously unknown strangers with Detective Warren calling the shots. Hmmmmmm, not sure if I'd like this.

For the first time in my life I started to get a real sense of what celebrities go through, never being left alone for a second and always having people to watch and judge your every move. This would be tougher than I'd thought, and these were just my thoughts in anticipation of the task force. Once the team was assembled I would realize that I'd totally underestimated the sense of suffocation I'd be experiencing.

[CHAPTER 31]

My first task force surprise was the fact that my two uniforms were, yep you guessed it, Donny's two high school buddies. Up until that point a small part of me had been relieved that I'd basically have my own personal bodyguards – no more risk and no more big scares. That was until I realized that my safety was reliant on the fast work and quick thinking of Frick and Frack. I was somewhat less than thrilled.

Then came surprise number two – Detective Warren would actually be one of the detectives on the task force. This was kind of my worst case scenario. I wouldn't be feeling perfectly safe from bodily harm based on my dynamic duo bodyguards, and I wouldn't have much latitude in terms of doing any proactive investigating with Warren breathing down my neck! I started to get a sinking feeling that I would end up on the periphery of this investigation with everyone else in the thick of the action. And honestly, I couldn't envision my menopausal self making any risky and melodramatic action moves to lose my tail so that I could jump into the fray and solve the murder single-handedly. That kind of thing just didn't sound like me – even to me.

I was also starting to get concerned that my task force might drive away others who would normally be eager to share any new information, and I certainly couldn't see Warren confiding in me herself. That might happen in the movies, but a true professional does not spill her guts to an amateur any more than a true marketing professional would reveal prioritary details of a client's campaign to an outsider. What the hell. Seemed like a good time to go to my office and get some work done.

To my great relief, Frick and Frack stationed themselves barely within my sight and not up my nose as I had feared. I was pretty sure they would not even be able to overhear a phone conversation – so I started feeling a bit more at ease. Prior to leaving, Warren had alerted me that the full task force would meet back at my office at eleven that morning. They would be prepared to debrief me with the assumption that I was somehow a key player in the killer's mind. I have to admit that did seem intriguing to me. Okay, maybe Clovis wasn't the only one who liked a little attention now and then.

I gave some thought to making a few "unapproved by police" phone calls, but decided it was too early to start pissing off the whole task force. I spent the next 45 minutes or so, until eleven, doing actual agency work. I signed a bunch of things and reviewed and commented on a bunch more. By eleven, I really felt as though I actually worked at this place and didn't just drop in sporadically whenever I was in search of people looking for a reason to gab about the murder. It was amazing how quickly you could get yourself recharged and reinvigorated. It helps that the work we do is really very interesting. How do people in boring jobs do it?

At eleven on the nose, my bodyguards arrived to escort me to the Portfolio Room for my debriefing. Better not get used to the diva treatment – I was sure it wouldn't last very long. I wondered how it would work when I had to go to the bathroom for the first time. Why does my mind always go to the strangest places?

As we entered the Portfolio Room I could see that we were the last to arrive. My four detectives were all present and accounted for and in the process of helping themselves to giant Styrofoam tumblers of coffee and bear claws from the built-in buffet along the entry wall. God bless Peg, she'd spotted the team and fixed them all up with her usual brand of incredibly engaging hospitality. You'd think it was her job! The wall opposite the buffet was a dramatic curve of floor to ceiling glass flanked by built-in cabinets to house the requisite presentation technology. Overall it was a simple yet elegant setting.

After multiple murmurings about Peg and sainthood, the crew began to settle down and the debriefing got underway. The crew was Warren and Schultz investigating me and Carpenter and Davenport checking out my acquaintances, and, of course, my ever vigilant bodyguards – Itchy and Scratchy – why could I never remember their names? Warren started with an overview of my life since moving from Connecticut to Omaha. Holy crap – she sure knew a lot about me. I had a momentary twinge over whether or not I'd done anything to embarrass myself publicly – they had clearly left no stone unturned.

As Warren concluded her overview – guess my life'd been

more boring than I'd realized – I started to wonder what, if anything, they'd have to ask me. No need. I was about to find out that they had classified my acquaintances into six categories: colleagues acquainted directly through business (clients, co-workers, vendors) who knew and who may or may not have known Claire; acquaintances I had known through community activities (ones with whom I'd served on various boards, or met in ad community circumstances that were not directly related to my business – including our competitors.) This category was also broken down into those who did know Claire and others who may or may not have known Claire; and finally, my personal friends broken down into those who did or didn't know Claire. I think they got everybody.

The initial discussion revolved around the ones who definitely knew Claire and which ones rose to the top as being even remotely capable of murder. Naturally, Clovis made it to the top even though forensics ruled her out. The process of elimination was very important in order to think this thing through flawlessly. I was actually very impressed with the methodical way in which the investigation was conducted – these were not sloppy cops by any stretch of the imagination. They brought up a few points that really made me sit up and take notice. In advertising and marketing we tend to think of ourselves as pure thinkers, and often we are, but we are also fairly quick to discount the pure thinking power of virtually anyone else. Once in a while we needed a gentle reminder that there were others who knew how to think, and getting a very different perspective was certainly eye opening.

By the time we neared conclusion of our initial debriefing

we had a list of likely candidates and a list of unlikely but not out-of-the-woods candidates. It was a long list. I did not envy Detectives Carpenter and Davenport. We spent another half an hour speculating on each candidate and various evidentiary possibilities.

One such candidate was a client by the name of Trixie. Both Claire and I had worked with Trixie – she as the day-to-day account person and I as the media specialist. Trixie could be really nice and she could be a firecracker next to a heating stove. You just never knew.

Ironically, after all of Claire's machinations to keep Trixie in a constantly pacified state – and trust me it was something she worked really hard at – we learned over time that the most effective way of keeping Trixie in a perpetual good mood was to trot some cute guys in front of her. One day Trixie loved the ad we presented and its brilliant strategic direction and the next day she was claiming that the copy didn't even make sense. Then in would walk a cute art director and suddenly everything was back to brilliant!! A good looking guy certainly went a long way with Trixie. You'd think we'd have learned over the years – but we honestly never made the connection between Trixie's love of our work and whether or not she heard it from a gorgeous young hunk until the final round. Can you say cougar?

After Claire's years of serious hustling to mollify Trixie 24/7, things came to an explosive and abrupt end one sunny day. Trixie had seen our latest ad campaign and she'd gushed over it like no other. This was by far the best she'd ever seen. There were one or two minor tweaks to be made and she was ready to sign off. We agreed to stop into her office the next day after revisions were complete to finalize the ad and discuss the media where it would be running, which is why I was invited. Little did we realize that Claire and I had been set up to be proverbial lambs led to the slaughter.

Early the next morning, prior to leaving for Trixie's office, we learned that Sonny, our happy go lucky, and very flirty art director, had given his notice. Oh crap, he was Trixie's favorite. Claire broke out into a cold sweat at the very thought of having to break this news to her volatile client. At that juncture I realized we'd never have time to discuss the media campaign for the new ads so there was really no reason for me to go along. But sensing Claire's trepidation, I agreed to accompany her as moral support primarily because I was afraid she would crack and embarrass the company. Frankly, without some serious support I had grave doubts as to whether Claire would have the wherewithal to make it over to Trixie's at all that day, but make it she did.

Upon our arrival we were ushered immediately into Trixie's office by a new, young assistant who appeared to have some sort of palsy. That should have been our first clue. We no sooner plunked our butts in Trixie's 1950s office chairs (these were not retro – they were actual 1950s chairs replete with grimy, tacky fabric and a little bit of rust to keep them from swiveling easily) when we realized by the look on her face that Sonny must have scooped us and called ahead with his news. Shit.

Just as Claire was about to open her mouth the lion roared. She roared and roared and then she roared some more. For a petite little waif of a woman she sure could crank up the volume. Had it not been the heat of the battle I could have found amusement in the

175

visual discrepancy of seeing this tiny screaming howler monkey turning big old Claire into a quivering bowl of mush. Mid-roar, Claire and I realized we'd been given a clear and loud command to leave. She didn't have to tell us twice. We nearly trampled each other in our frantic efforts to bolt out of the front door. I'm guessing our tumultuous exit was fuel for water cooler humor for quite some time.

Once outside I immediately began to see the amusing aspects of our recent encounter and I proceeded to laugh uncontrollably for what seemed like an hour or two. I guess my laughter was all that Claire needed because she instantly burst into tears with the same unending emotional supply as my laughter seemed to exhibit, and there we stood in Trixie's busy parking lot laughing and crying hysterically.

Once able to get myself under control I focused on comforting Claire. But she was not to be comforted. I ushered her into the car and drove to the nearest restaurant just to get us out of the line of fire should Trixie have had a chance to reload her cannon. Claire continued sobbing pitiably. Once able to catch her breath Claire pointed to the restaurant and said, "drink."

We went inside and ordered our drinks. Claire pointed at me and uttered one final word, "talk."

So we drank, I talked and she quietly cried. After about two hours we just gave up, paid the bill and went home. But Claire never truly recovered from her humiliating experience. She lived to taunt and backstab Trixie at every opportunity. In fact she even manufactured a few opportunities to make Trixie look bad. Recently Trixie had been let go from her lucrative position – and word on the street was that she was not a happy camper.

Trixie ranked high up on our new list of suspects since I was the only one left who knew all of the details of her ridiculous antics and I would be the one most likely to point the finger at her. This exercise was proving to be very interesting. Unfortunately Claire's career had fostered more of these dysfunctional relationships than you could begin to imagine, and I was beginning to realize that I was in a position to have observed many of them.

After hours of exploring and examining, we all agreed that the list was complete, and I was exhausted. The detectives packed up and left me to my personal detail. I was ready to go home – end of day or not. It is surprising how much more tiring a session can be when there is an ever present threat to one's own safety in the wings. I suggested to my "guys" that they could accompany me home and head on out themselves. That's when they informed me that they had strict instructions from Donny who was determined to conduct his own debriefing session immediately following the detectives' departure, and he was expecting me there. Oh crap. I was not in the mood. But Donny was not to be deterred.

As I watched Donny enter the conference room full of vim and vigor and ready to get down to the business of the hunt, my life – and evening – flashed briefly through my mind. Better to just go along placidly – any objections would only serve to prolong my Donny-imposed imprisonment. Shortly after Donny's arrival some of his team members sauntered in: Clarke Holmes, our acerbic creative director and Lois Lang, one of our bright young project directors. I knew there were at least two others on Donny's team, but apparently they were crashing on a tight deadline and would not be able to join us. So we began.

To my surprise, once Donny asked to be briefed on the list, his high school buddies/my protectors took over entirely. I was impressed. There'd been no snoozing on the part of my bodyguards – they knew every detail on that list backward and forward.

That's when Donny's team went into action so I got to just hang out and listen to them interact. As Donny's buddies completed their exemplary police report, I sat back and watched the brain power move into action. Donny and his team members took our initial compilation and proceeded to work it and mold it and add viewpoints and angles that neither I nor the trained detectives had even considered. They began to refine and shape the data in such a way that it would be much easier to formulate interview questions and either confirm or eliminate each person on the list as a likely suspect.

I have to say I was most impressed. We've been known to boast about the quality of our thinking and our legendary problem solving skills, and I see evidence of that in some form every day. But sometimes it takes a non-work-related exercise to remind me of just how sharp these people really are.

The excercise appeared to give Donny's group the upper hand in the team challenge. And the more we examined the information surrounding Claire's and my relationship with the various characters on the list, the more it became evident that my presence in the whole murder equation would absolutely help the police in narrowing the suspect list. The murderer had had interaction with both Claire and me and was worrying that I was nosing around in dangerous areas.

Everyone in the room was jubilant – except me. They could see the light at the end of the tunnel and they smelled victory. Even the two cops were anxious to get their report filed and in the hands of Warren. This investigation was finally starting to take shape.

Problem was – the shape it was taking led firmly in my direction. What had been a vague notion earlier in the day was now becoming hard and jarringly convincing evidence. And that took my personal safety threat level from orange to red. No longer was I satisfied to have my bodyguards deposit me at my door for the night. I was flat out scared.

I didn't need to worry though. My cops had no intention of deserting me for the night. As the three of us arrived at my doorstep we were greeted by my nighttime detail, Johnson and Brainerd. We all went inside for a cup of coffee and an opportunity to get comfortable around one another. After all, we were facing a potential life-and-death situation.

Meeting the guys also helped to alleviate Jon's concerns. As I had briefed him on the day's events, he had become increasing agitated over our safety. After our little coffee klatch we were all pretty satisfied with the security measures. Just as the on duty guys were getting ready to shove off: Johnson for our family room and Brainerd for a car parked across the street from our house, and the ever vigilant Frick and Frack, who turned out to be Riley and O'Dowd, once I made an effort to pay attention to their names, were ready to go off duty for the night, my phone rang.

[CHAPTER 32]

Jon grabbed the receiver, listened and handed it to me with a face of apology. It was Clovis. Oh god.

"Donna, Donna," Clovis began. I could see this was going to be slightly less pleasant than a cold water enema.

"Donna," Clovis continued, "I heard a rumor that was most distressing and I wanted to call so you could tell me it's not true." The sound of anguish in her voice was palpable.

"God Clovis, did someone else get murdered?" I clamored in response to her obvious dismay.

"No Donna, worse," she proclaimed emphatically.

Worse than someone else getting murdered? What? Did Claire come back to life as a zombie to terrorize the villagers?

"Clovis," I demanded, "Tell me what happened!"

"Donna, I heard that the police have decided you're the key to finding the murderer." Clovis blurted inconsolably, "My sources even said that you have a 24-hour guard detail. Please please tell me that isn't true, Donna."

Of course, what would be worse than a second murder to Clovis? Elementary, not being the center of attention. I was really beginning to think that the only thing that would satisfy her would be to make her the murder victim, and it was getting more tempting by the minute. But, of course, being the second murder victim just wouldn't do. How inconsiderate of Claire to take first honors away from her. My reverie came to a close with a keening animal sound coming out of the phone. This woman was really in pain.

"Clovis," I began.

"Donna, " she interrupted, "I know this thing revolves around me. I know things. After all I have pure Romanian gypsy blood running through my veins. "

"Yes, Clovis," I responded.

"And that ridiculous Detective Warren said that they were done talking to me for now. She told me not to bother checking in five times a day anymore," Clovis sputtered.

Oh god, now she was gonna cry. The last thing I wanted to be doing tonight was to comfort this screaming lunatic. But, I knew if I couldn't say something to satisfy her I'd be on the phone until sunrise. Either that or the urge to kill her would cease to be a distant fantasy and start to become my life's mission. And that could start getting unpleasant for me.

"Look Clovis," I offered, "you and Claire and I knew a lot of people in common. It's certainly possible that you and I are both the link, it's just that the detectives have focused on me because of the threatening notes."

"You bring up another good point, Donna, " Clovis proceeded

in an injured voice, "Why did you get those notes and not me? I'm just as involved in this investigation as you are – in fact at the risk of patting myself on the back I think it's essential to admit that I've actually done quite a bit more to help the police than you have. Now don't try to deny it, Donna, I know how you love to be the center of attention all the time, but sometimes you have to move over and make room for someone more capable. There, I've said it – it needed to be said," Clovis ended with a note of triumph.

"Ya know, Clovis, I didn't exactly ask to be singled out by the killer," I offered wearily.

"I suppose that's true, Donna. When you put it like that I can feel more charitable toward your pathetic attempt for attention – you know everybody's talking about it – but yes, I can see that you probably weren't directly responsible for being the recipient of the threatening notes," Clovis allowed. "And I would agree that the killer probably did have interaction with both of us – and probably even Claire for that matter. "

"Yes, Clovis, now I think you're getting somewhere," I gently suggested in the same manner in which I would speak to an errant five year old. This experience was teaching me patience like I'd never known. I was not in a business where patience was often considered a virtue. We were hard driving and fast paced. We raced ahead and took no prisoners. This was kind of new for me. I was showing kindness to a sanity-challenged individual and it was proving to take more discipline than I'd thought.

"And Donna," Clovis continued, "you'd better tell those policemen that I'll be expecting my bodyguards within the next half an hour."

Oh shit. I looked up at my four protectors and saw that they were reading my body language. Within a split second you could see from every one of their demeanors that they knew exactly what Clovis had demanded and they were thinking, "Oh shit." Before I had a chance to recover, all four men bolted out of my front door. Riley and O'Dowd on their way home and Johnson and Brainerd both into the awaiting parked car, I guess Johnson figured that his exposure to danger in an isolated parked car would be safer than my family room with the ever looming threat of a Clovis attack.

A few more seconds and a deep breath and I was able to say without impunity, "Clovis, I don't have any police guards here right now. You'll have to take that up with Detective Warren."

"Really," she responded. "Well, that doesn't track with my recent intelligence, but I'll have to take your word for it, Donna."

And just like that she was off the phone. I turned to Jon who looked on in amazement.

"Donna," he ventured, "How does she know everything like that?"

"Jon," I responded even more wearily than before, "I have no idea how that woman does any of the things that she does. She is one of the true mysteries of life."

After a lovely but quick meal prepared by Jon, I headed straight up for bed. I figured with my life in official jeopardy I'd probably only sleep in fits and starts – so I'd better get a jump on it. Besides I'd been having a few nights of menopausal insomnia even before Claire's murder, so with the added drama of impending death I didn't think a serene night's sleep was in my foreseeable future. Although I was trying a new natural sleep aid recommended by my chiropractor, I figured it probably wouldn't be strong enough to counter the caffeine jolt effect that usually resulted from any nighttime exposure to Clovis.

[CHAPTER 33]

The next morning Liv flew into my office bright and early.

"Hey Donna, how're you doing?" she began.

Before I had a chance to respond, "My team has been very busy with some of the new information on Claire's murder. You know Lake, he's got such an analytical brain. We've come to the conclusion that the police have a good point about the murderer being someone who's well acquainted with both you and Claire. But we also think the murderer knows Clovis fairly well."

I sat back a little surprised.

"I won't bore you with all of Lake's analytical hypothesis, but as a team we've reviewed his findings and believe that he's really on to something. I've already spoken to Warren and she agrees."

My heart stopped beating. Oh god, please don't tell me that Warren would make me stay with Clovis so that we could both be protected by the same crew. That would be a punishment too great even if I had been the murderer. No one deserves that kind of torture.

Liv could see immediately that I was about to erupt into uncontrolled violence or hysterical sobbing. Just as she was about to dispel my fears, Kyle walked into my office.

"Hey guys," he started, "just heard from Clovis. She's happier than she's been since I've known her. The police have assigned her a bodyguard detail and she spent fifteen minutes complaining to me about her lack of privacy and the invasion in her life – she is absolutely elated."

Liv and I looked at each other and shrugged. I felt as though I'd just dodged a major bullet.

Kyle went on, "Clovis actually brought up a good point."

Now Liv and I glanced at each other with uncertainty – had we both just entered into the twilight zone? It looked like Kyle but it sure as hell didn't sound like anything we'd ever heard coming out of Kyle's mouth. Sensing our consternation Kyle shrugged and went on.

"Remember the author of that stupid self-help book? You know the one where the main premise was that women are like kitchen appliances?" he pressed on.

Yeah, of course we remembered. It was nothing short of ridiculous and Claire, in a ludicrous attempt to convince Donny that she was our primary new business leader, had agreed to our extreme dismay, that we'd promote the stupid book. The woman had proved to be more ridiculous than her book – which was a feat in and of itself – and we were forced, after several painfully embarrassing attempts to arrive at a strategic direction, to politely suggest that she find the magical promotional elixir she sought elsewhere. It was just torture and another good reason for Claire's hasty move to the outdoor company. Well, maybe not terribly good for those poor slobs at Toto - but undeniably good for us.

But our "You too are like a Waring blender" author did not sever her relationship until she had had a run-in with both Clovis and me. Clovis had told her that we could not begin to promote her unless she agreed to a complete redesign of her hideously bad "fifties, with no chance of being trendy and camp" book jacket. Apparently said jacket had been designed and implemented by her ailing father – a man who had been neither a designer nor a photographer, but who had had some of his best days in the 50s. Needless to say, our hypersensitive author had been incensed by Clovis' brutal honesty. Figures, the one time Clovis is dead-on about anything, it causes a Mt. St. Helens response from our "possibly even crazier than Clovis" client.

In my case it was a simple, here's what we've done for you and we expect you to pay your bill. It was a very small invoice – since we hadn't gotten very far – but her injured sensibilities told her that she owed us nothing. After several weeks of rational discussion – none of which emanated from her – she grudgingly remitted her check with a note telling me what I could do with it. Had I chosen to follow her graphic directions I would certainly have made it into Ripley's!

It was apparently Clovis' contention that the blender-lady was our most likely candidate since her anger at Claire for causing all of her humiliation far outweighed any negative feelings she had about the other two of us. I had to admit, Clovis had a point. On the other hand if the blender-lady was that nuts – and I absolutely believed she was – there was a good chance she was gearing up to nail both Clovis and me. Great, I was sure tonight's nightmares would feature at least one angry kitchen appliance.

Now, Kyle was getting to the main point of his visit. Clovis wanted us to track down blender-lady and smoke her out. She wanted a Marcel road trip and she wanted to be the main attraction. Liv and I just looked at each other warily, and then the three of us shrugged. A road trip it would be.

The way I looked at it, if blender-lady was the killer I would never be safer than surrounded by: my two bodyguards; Clovis, proving that fear had really messed up my head because I typically never felt safe around that lunatic, and her two bodyguards; Liv and Kyle and last but not least: Babs and Peg, since they are probably the only two people in the world who can handle Clovis when she's in rare form – which is usually. Since we'd all gotten in early that morning we decided to set out immediately. Clovis and her posse met us on the corner of 114th and Dodge and we all proceeded to the little office that blender-lady had rented in Regency.

As luck would have it blender-lady, Camille DeVille, was sitting behind her desk checking her morning e-mails when our caravan arrived. There she sat in all her mid-life glory, clothed in her fifties wardrobe (and not in a cool retro fifties way,) and her matching fifties hairdo. As we began to pile in we pretty much filled up her whole office and evidently scared the crap out of her. She arose from behind her Louis the XIV desk with a chortling and rasping sound as her face and neck turned from rapidly deepening shades of reddish magenta into a deep purple. Hmmm, I'm not a cop but she sure looked guilty to me. I was all for slapping the cuffs on her and hauling her into the station for questioning. Admittedly I was starting to get a little sick of the high drama all the time.

We waited until Ms. DeVille got herself back under control.

"I will have to ask that you leave my premises immediately," she began in an imperious and disdainful manner. "You may imagine that you are hardly welcome here."

Her little white fluffy dog jumped down from his perch on her matching Louis the XIV chaise and proceeded to bite Riley on the ankle. As the blood dribbled onto the white and blue tulle fabric Riley crumpled to the floor in pain. Just at that moment DeVille reached into her desk for what the cops clearly thought was a deadly weapon. Guns were drawn, civilians ducked (which was damn hard to do in that cramped space) and we had clearly moved past threat level red.

No one moved. O'Dowd began addressing DeVille in an authoritative and commanding tone.

"Ma'am, drop your weapon and put your hands above your head." He started slowly and firmly.

"Oh don't be ridiculous officer," she countered as she pulled her hand out of the drawer with an aerosol can of Neosporin and a box of band-aids. "It will just take me a minute to patch this poor officer so you can all be on your way." She bustled about.

Thank God for the training that made these guards hold their fire or this could have been a repeat of the St. Valentine's Day massacre. Not only had she ignored all of the dire warnings, DeVille had seemed to be oblivious to the fact that anyone else was in the room.

She had another in a long line of fluffy dog related injuries to attend to and nothing could deter her. She promptly patched up Riley while O'Dowd and the others replaced their weapons to a chorus of multi-colored red faces. I couldn't tell if the festive facial coloring was more from anger or embarrassment – both were warranted.

Everyone stopped to take a few breaths. The desire to exit DeVille's office was palpable – no one wanted to be here, but we hadn't even begun to accomplish our desired task. Liv regained her composure first so she took the reins.

"Camille," she began methodically, "we're sorry to disturb you but there are a few questions that we need to ask you."

Before Liv had a chance to get any further she was interrupted by an unearthly screech.

"Look Camille," Clovis shrieked, clearly anxious to grab the attention away from Liv and place it firmly back on herself, "I have to know about your last conversation with Claire. I suppose you are aware that she has been brutally murdered and that I am under suspicion. It is my belief that you and Claire had..."

Just as Camille had begun to look up toward Clovis with an undeniable glint of murder in her eyes, Clovis was unceremoniously jostled out of the room by the perfectly executed ministrations of Babs and Peg. She was out the door and down the hall before she had a chance to hiccup. God bless those two – I started wondering how life might have been different had they been in some painfully embarrassing client meetings where Clovis had dropped one of her proverbial verbal lead balloons that caused all of us to quietly pray for Captain Kirk's voice ordering Scottie to "beam us up." Short of a miraculous rescue in the true Star Trek tradition, Clovis' spontaneous removal would have been the next best thing. However, no time for daydreaming now, it was imperative we got things back on track before we lost our witness forever.

Liv had begun to mollify Camille by apologizing for Clovis' erratic behavior. She explained that apparently Clovis had been closer to the murder victim than any of us had realized and she was starting to unravel – even more so than usual. Camille just shrugged. Clearly Clovis' legacy had preceded her. Should I be surprised?

By the time I was fully back in focus Liv had the situation under control. She and Camille were having a calm and rational conversation about her relationship with Claire and where things had stood at the time of the murder. Understandably, Camille did blame Claire for agreeing to take on her assignment when the rest of the agency was clearly not in sync with a product we could in no way support.

In fairness to Camille, in her own mind she was convinced her book was dynamite. So naturally she assumed that with a knowledgeable and professional agency she could be an overnight sensation. Hell, she even had a dress picked out for the celebration dinner honoring her book's first week on the New York Times best seller list.

Liv worked her way through the anger and disappointment and came up with a few issues that needed to be considered. She thanked Camille for her time and rapidly began ushering all of us back out to the parking lot. Once outside we saw Babs and Peg still wrestling with an overwrought Clovis.

"Fine," Clovis barked "Now we have no chance of getting at the truth. Liv doesn't have my inbred sense of detecting truth and evasion. I'm the only one who could really tell if DeVille is our woman. You two have just destroyed any chance.."

Seeing the rest of us heading toward them, Peg had only two words remaining for Clovis. "Shut it." Surprisingly she did, with barely a yelp.

Once reunited, Liv proceeded to explain that she thought DeVille a potential, but not highly likely suspect. She was clearly the right stature and strength – that Camille was a big girl. She also had the requisite anger toward Claire. Liv felt it wise to have Detective Warren check out her alibi, but her sense was that Camille was not our girl. She was able to drive this point home when she explained that DeVille had taken her book to two other agencies since her troubled experience with Marcel. One had thrown her out outright. They'd told her they'd have an easier time marketing g-strings to nuns. The other had genuinely tried to make some headway with her book.

They had been in financial straits and were willing to accept any business that came their way. After a month of desperately flailing about, even they had to admit that the book was virtually unmarketable. Liv's conclusion was that there would already be an enormous path of dead bodies had Camille succumbed to murdering everyone who wounded her pride in relation to the ill-fated book.

Clovis continued to rant about a potential argument between Claire and Camille. But since that was an out-and-out guess, although Clovis claimed her Romanian ancestry automatically transformed her guesses into fact, there was no way of knowing if any such argument had occurred. We agreed that Camille would remain on the list but we would not focus all of our attention on her.

[CHAPTER 34]

Back at the office we were ready to start the day's work.
Nothing like a shoot-out scare to get the old adrenalin flowing.
Kyle and I had a moment to reflect before moving forward with
our workday. My bodyguards were busily making their report to
Warren. Both Kyle and I felt that although we'd taken a back seat in
today's action, we were still much the worse for wear. We agreed to
avoid further gun activity at all cost.

We couldn't resist deciding on our next action steps before
heading off to our respective meetings. Donny would be seriously
pissed off that Liv's team seemed to be every bit up to speed on the
latest police findings.

We quietly pondered the three-way connection that seemed to
have captured everyone's attention. Was there another suspect with
a strong connection and personal knowledge of Claire, Clovis and
me? That check on DeVille's alibi would be a critical piece of data.

In the meantime, our thoughts immediately turned to employees
on the Marcel staff. Loathe as we were to suspect anyone in the

Marcel family, we had to admit that a close review of employees was the logical next step under the circumstances. I mean how could we not look at the people who were most likely to have involvement with all three of us – particularly considering the fact that so much of our work was conducted under a boatload of pressure. Seemed like a logical scenario for a murder, but man, would that suck. One thing we agreed on was that we'd have to review the facts discreetly between ourselves before alerting anyone else to our suspicions. Making a federal case out of this ultra sensitive part of the investigation could end up causing a rift with a decidedly negative impact on our corporate culture, and we could ill afford to do that.

Solemnly Kyle and I made a list of suspects from within our office. Although it would be fair to say that virtually everyone in the office had had a close connection to Claire, Clovis and me, there did seem to be a clear pattern emerging. Our list consisted only of staffers involved in major projects, accounts and new business pitches in which all three of us had a heavy involvement. On top of that we looked for incidents of turmoil and disruptive behavior. Oddly that added criteria only served to lengthen the list. It's actually not all that surprising for anyone who knew Clovis and Claire.

We continued to refine the list by eliminating close confidants of any of the three of us. Perhaps we were hasty in making these exclusions but it just felt right. After diligently working on our list for a half an hour we narrowed it down to three main possibilities.

Clarke, our Creative Director, had worked on several large new business pitches with all three of us, some we'd won and some had eluded us. One pitch in particular, to a large auto parts manufacturer, had caused an inordinate amount of grief between the four of us. What was highly unusual was the fact that Claire, Clovis and I were in agreement in our disagreement with Clarke.

It did seem as though Clarke's ego had been inordinately tied up in that particular pitch. He fought like a ninja and his logic seemed unaccountably flawed. Needless to say this was not one of our celebrated victories. We differed on direction, which cost us a great deal of time in the early stages but were able to rally the troops in time for the final presentation. Ironically, as with so many of these large dog and pony shows, the main contact realized at the eleventh hour that his brother-in-law in Poughkeepsie was a marketing expert. Instead of hiring an agency they hired the brother-in-law – who just happened to have a wife with an ad agency in White Plains. Will wonders never cease? They never do in the ad business!

Nothing could make me believe that Clarke was a killer – even though Claire said some things to Clarke during that pitch that would have made me want to rap her over the head. Clarke had too much integrity to leave her dead body on the ground and head for the hills. I had to imagine that even supposing he'd become overwrought and struck her fatally, Clarke would have called 911 and blamed himself piteously. I couldn't be that wrong about a person's character. It would, however, be interesting to delve a little deeper into why this particular project had clearly been so inflammatory to Clarke.

Then there was Maddy in accounting, a little scrap of a girl with a chest large enough to need its own zip code. She was quiet and diligent, but you never wanted her to dislike you. Maddy disliked quite a few people but none with quite the level of intensity as her open hostility toward Claire. She would take any shot at Claire that she could. Every invoice that Claire's work generated was scrutinized with a magnifying glass, every expense report was questioned endlessly. And every time Maddy thought she had the minutest of discrepancies she marched into Donny's office with a puffed up, overzealous pride reminiscent of the cat who swallowed the canary. On such occasions Donny would review the information and either question Claire for clarification or send Maddy back to her office in a financial walk of shame. Maddy worked so hard to torment Claire, yet rarely did any of these incidents erupt in the publicly searing humiliation that she had so eagerly sought for Claire, who wasn't dumb enough to ruin her reputation by doing anything too obvious.

Now everyone knew that Maddy had it in for Claire, and what was starting to surface was the fact that before departing from Marcel, Claire had used every device within her power to try and oust Maddy. Honestly, Claire was no easy opponent. I had to give Maddy credit though. Once she'd made her mind up that Claire was a rotter she was not about to back down no matter how great the threat. They provided endless hours of entertainment for anyone drawn to bloody and ruthless verbal bludgeoning.

Their sordid history did arouse suspicions as to whether or not Maddy and Claire might have met outside of the Boy Scout dinner reviving ancient and deep seated hostilities. Who knows, after a drink or two Maddy might well be tempted to clobber that nasty guttersnipe. I could certainly understand the temptation. Conversely, I could also understand Maddy's reluctance to spend a lifetime in jail for ridding the world of a bad seed. Although Maddy's diminutive stature suggested she was not a likely suspect we felt compelled to examine the path of excessive hostility between the two women.

And finally, we had to address our lovable IT guy, Mark. Mark was tall and lean with a light brown buzz cut. He casually sauntered around the office in cut-offs and sandals, and he favored the foosball table for stress-reducing therapy. There had been that one day when the three of us, Claire, Clovis and I, were battling for the same equipment, each for our own presentations. For one flimsy reason or another, none of us had thought ahead and reserved the proper components as was standard procedure and we were all begging for our lives at the last minute. Mark, as is his way, was trying to figure out how to make us all winners rather than leave two of us losers. We were all spoiled and used to Mark pulling rabbits out of his hat for us on a regular basis. But this time it wasn't going to be that easy. Some of our electronics were out for repair and some were already in use.

Claire had had no time for that. She planned on being the winner and had begun her verbal assault of Mark the moment the realization dawned that getting the equipment she needed was not a certainty. The poor guy never had a chance. He was trying to work out the best arrangement while she stood nearby to harangue him with a constant and unrelenting stream of abuse. As people walked by, she took great pains to assure them that the idiot Mark was incapable of running his department and doling out equipment as needed. Somehow the fact that Mark was not the one at fault never made it into her diatribe.

Clovis had taken a more surreptitious approach and was texting poor Mark relentlessly. Her barbs were no less pointed – they were just written versus being shared openly with the whole office. So on top of Claire's constant barrage was a fairly constant pinging to advise him of yet another text. As for me, I had asked once and was awaiting the fateful conclusion which would undoubtedly be better than I deserved for not having organized my presentation tools better. Mark had never let me down before – but I was hard pressed to see how he would make this work. Although I took pride in the fact that I was not proactively adding to the ongoing maelstrom, I was painfully aware that my involvement served to make things that much more difficult for Mark. Hell, he was surrounded by the witches of Eastwick and one wrong move on his part would bring our collective wrath down on the innocent villagers. That's a lot of responsibility. And he certainly knew I was in the middle of the fray with or without continual reminders from me.

But even considering all the horrors that befell him that day, I can't imagine Mark losing his temper in a murderous rampage outside of a Boy Scout's dinner. If he didn't kill the shrieking harridan on the infamous day of the electronics debacle, I was guessing he was clean as a whistle. I do know that although Mark worked things out so that everyone had what they needed for their presentation, Claire never stopped baiting him and berating him in front of others through all the rest of her days at Marcel. She never forgave him for giving her the older of our two projectors on that fateful day. He may have been quiet but Mark knew how to get his shots in, in a way that counted.

And now it occurs to me that Mark's equipment has some pretty odd shapes, and fairly heavy components. God, I hated to even think it, but could that account for the odd shape of the fatal wound?

Just as we were wrapping up our list and all of the corresponding details, our men in blue walked into the room. At that point Kyle and I took a few more minutes to brief them on our thoughts about our three most likely staffers. Riley and O'Dowd jumped on the phone to rebrief Warren. As Kyle and I took our leave I noticed a sizeable bandage peeking out of Riley's sock. Ouch, that must have been one nasty bite.

Kyle ran to a meeting while I returned to my office to make some overdue phone calls. I was starting to feel the pressure of spending way too much time entrenched in this murder investigation. At first it was a choice, but now I was just caught up in the momentum, and it felt a lot like being dragged under a car – not that I've ever actually experienced that particular ordeal.

[CHAPTER 35]

At lunch time I was fully prepared to grab a quick bite and read some articles that had been piling up on my desk. It was time to take a break from murder and mayhem. I was just making my final decision on where to grab lunch – either HyVee or Subway, when Liv flew into my office.

"Come on Donna, let's go," she commanded.

"Go where?" I replied with a puzzled frown.

"Lacy called. She's all upset because Garth dumped her. She's in need of consolation and somehow thinks I'm her new best friend. Sheesh, the things I do for you, Donna," Liv blurted.

"Me, how do you figure?" I barked, running behind Liv as I grabbed my purse on the way out.

"You're the one that got me into this whole thing and now I've got to do the thing you know I hate most, pretend I care about her lonely-heart rantings," Liv snapped. "I'd say this is definitely your doing – so you get to come with me."

We grabbed my bodyguards on the way out of the building and

headed over to Biaggi's. I usually preferred the food at Charleston's for these quick business lunches, but the noise factor was deafening and my bodyguards were not about to fight the crowds trying to keep me safe. Hell, in reality I would have far preferred an elegant lunch at Le Voltaire, or one of the many other chef-owned treasures we were fortunate enough to have in Omaha. But, some days the focus was more on business than on the dining experience, and the fact was, my safety detail was not all that thrilled about a public lunch at all, so I figured I'd better not push my luck. I do think they could see that I was starting to go stir crazy. This little outing would kill two birds with one stone. Liv had managed to reach Lacy on the way out.

"All set, Lace," Liv started. "We'll meet you at Biaggi's in five."

Both Biaggi's and Charleston's were a stone's throw from the Marcel offices so it was no big deal. It was likely that Lacy would not be eating much anyway. Once in the restaurant Liv asked for an enclosed table near one of the windows. There were advantages in that it was more private and secluded than most tables, yet you weren't sitting intimately together in a booth – everyone got her own chair. The Tuscan motif with sunny faux-painted walls, heavy earth-toned window treatments and thick bronze light fixtures provided a cozy setting for our little tete-a-tete. The boys flashed their badges and got the semi-secluded window table next to ours which they liked since they had a bird's-eye view of everything in the place.

We were only seated for about three minutes when Lacy made her puffy-eyed entrance. Geez, I hoped she had the day off. I sure as hell wouldn't want anyone to see me looking like that. She looked at me slightly askance as she seated herself next to Liv. I started hoping that Liv hadn't sprung me as a surprise – dumped women tend to hate surprises.

To my relief Liv had suggested that I come along since I am sort of an armchair psychiatrist around the office. At this point Lacy was desperate enough to try anything that might help. I had to admit I felt kind of sorry for her. I mean she was trapped working with the guy who'd just dumped her, she didn't know if either he or she would be accused of murdering his wife, and Lacy's existence alone gave them both a perfect motive. She had to be feeling as though everything were upside down, and that's never fun.

I figured I'd just sit back and let Liv and Lacy talk it out. I mean, I didn't know her at all and she probably would not appreciate interference from me. She'd made her choice and called Liv for advice. The best thing I could do would be to sit back and let them work things through. As I waited for the diatribe to begin I couldn't help but glance at Lacy. She was absolutely stunning, not at all like Claire. She had a perfect figure and she really knew how to wear the latest fashions. It wasn't difficult to see what Garth saw in her. Apparently Liv was more than willing to let Lacy get the ball rolling. She sat back looking convincingly sympathetic to our luncheon companion.

"So, Donna," Lacy began, "Liv tells me you're something of an expert in human behavior and relationships."

She was good. I never saw it coming. Damn Liv! And now I was trapped like a rat in a hole. Oh well, when in doubt, rely on your natural gift – BS.

"Well, Lacy," I responded, "I don't know that I'd go as far as to say I'm an expert."

"This is no time to be modest, Donna." Lacy demanded, "I'm fighting for my life here so let's not waste any more time. Okay?"

"Well sure Lacy." I sputtered meekly, realizing I was inextricably nailed, "Why don't you tell me what's going on with you."

"Well Donna," she began in earnest, "Garth started acting really funny within the past three or four days. I noticed it, but just figured it was brought on by everything he was going through and his concerns over his son. This morning we had breakfast and he told me that we were putting everything on permanent hold. No wedding, no living together; in fact, even dating casually was more than he could handle at this point." She sniffled, pulled a tissue out of her purse and started dabbing at her eyes.

"Okay," I enunciated slowly, "what do you think happened to make him change like that?"

"I think the old lady got to him. Y'know, his mother-in-law," Lacy snarled.

"Why only now?" I countered inquisitively, Liv shot me a ten volt "why are you making this worse" look.

"Well, the boy and his grandpa went out together the other night, and the two of them had dinner alone." Lacy began to gain steam as it gradually dawned on her that she really did know the origin of the problem and could more than likely find an easy solution. After all, a "hot and steamy" lady love beat mother-in-law logic pretty much anytime. Lacy was clearly starting to perk up.

"Makes sense," I reasoned in my best, yes I really do have the "creds voice." I was starting to feel pretty cocky.

"Y'know," Lacy continued, "I was expecting that awful woman to pull something like this. And I knew that Garth would be really vulnerable to this kind of attack. It just caught me off guard is all. Wow, I'm starting to feel much better."

I shot my best "and yet you doubt me" look at Liv and she just shrugged.

"The bitch," Lacy snarled angrily, "I'll just beat that old battle-ax at her own game."

This time Liv and I shared frightened glances. Had we created a monster?

"Oh hey, Lace," Liv ventured. "Maybe you should hang back on any involvement with Claire's mom. I mean with what she's been through and all you wouldn't get much sympathy for going after her."

"No no, Liv," Lacy reassured her with a slightly demonic look in her eye. "You misunderstand my meaning. I'm not going after the old bat publicly. This is a private battle between the two of us. Between you and me, she doesn't stand a ghost of a chance. Oh that's pretty funny, get it, she doesn't stand a ghost of a chance – kinda like her daughter."

At this point Liv and I were both seriously freaked out. This chick had murder written all over her. We weren't sure whether to try and reason with her or just run for our lives. I could tell by the look on Liv's face that the "run for our lives" option was winning. Even though we'd only had salads at this point I could tell that an "Oh shit, I forgot I had this meeting" excuse was about to pop out of

Liv's mouth. Before I could try and stop Liv, the silence was broken by Lacy as she continued her maniacal monologue.

"Oh yes," she gushed, "Our darling little mommy-in-law has no idea who she's messing with. I will pound her into dust and mix it with my breakfast milkshake."

Now I was ready to plead the forgotten-meeting excuse, and I was merely looking for a break in the crazy to get in there before Liv beat me to it. No need. Lacy announced that she was way too busy to finish lunch and picking herself up she left a couple of bills on the table, smiled in a profoundly chilling way, and marched out of the restaurant. Liv and I just sat with our mouths hanging open. The two female business geniuses, unable to muster an intelligible phrase. Before either of us had recovered we saw Riley's head pop up over the partition.

"What the fu…" he started and O'Dowd took up the reins. "..That bitch is nuts!"

Liv and I looked at each other, yep, mouths still hanging open. I was starting to think, but my body hadn't caught up with my brain. Riley and O'Dowd joined us at our table. They looked as disturbed as Liv and I. I felt a little better.

"Do you think?" I tentatively suggested.

"Don't look good," O'Dowd replied.

"Well, just because, I mean," Liv started, "people talk funny, doesn't mean…"

"Yeah, I know what you're sayin'." Riley agreed.

We sounded a lot like the gang who couldn't shoot straight. It was kind of embarrassing. The waitress came over and registered surprise at our losing a diner and joining tables with our neighbors. We could do little more than shrug at this point. Liv was anxious to get out. She'd had enough and she wasn't up to eating. I was starving. Yes, I was unnerved – but I still had to eat, didn't I? The boys were hungry too. So the three of us ordered a boatload of comfort food and Liv had a cup of coffee – after going outside for a quick cigarette.

It took a whole plate of gloppy baked rigatoni and a heaping plate of french fries before I started to feel human again. So sue me – comfort food has magical powers. The boys kept up with my every bite and Liv went through three cups of regular, a double espresso, and more cigarette breaks before we were all feeling copacetic. I'd have to remember not to have lunch with Liv again soon – it was just not good for my diet!

By the end of our marathon lunch we'd all agreed to a few things. The boys would let Warren know about our weird encounter with Lacy and then we'd all move on to other things. Far be it for us to place her on our suspect list just because she had a great motive and she was clearly certifiable. One cannot assume. Nor can one continue to interact with the certifiable - and remain unscathed!

[CHAPTER 36]

Back at the office again, and in recovery mode from some hauntingly disturbing events, I took a few deep cleansing breaths. If I survived this murder investigation, we were talking years of therapy to nullify the effects of virtually every aspect of this case. Thank god, solving murders was merely my pastime and not my career choice. This stuff really takes its toll.

I went in search of Kyle to fill him in on our latest adventures. Donny ran by with a high five. He was having way too much fun with this whole thing – and those buddies of his could not keep their mouths shut to save their lives! I should have figured.

When I finally found Kyle he was most concerned. Now that he was feeling an affinity for Garth he felt compelled to call and warn his new buddy of the coming apocalypse. Try as I might I could not convince Kyle that he did NOT want to be in the middle of this little love triangle. No one is more averse to snooping than Kyle, but he's also the most loyal friend that you could have. It was pointless. He could not ignore this issue without a word of caution to his friend, and the fact that there was an innocent young boy involved made him all the more determined. I had to admit – he was fearless. So I left him to it. I went back to my office with my head hanging kind of low. I realized that I had not done Kyle any favors by sharing my latest news, but the thought of hiding anything from Kyle seemed wrong. I knew if the situation were in reverse he'd have briefed me. So I had to be satisfied that I wasn't the cause of what would likely be Lacy's angry assault on Kyle, and I had to hope that her anger did not branch out to include me. Boy did I hope.

I swung by Liv's office to make sure that her recovery was complete. God bless her, she was smack in the middle of a conference call and I could tell that our lunch encounter was over and done – she had moved on. No one could throw themselves into their work like Liv, and when she did she was always at the top of her game. There was no fumbling and fussing because she'd had a bit of a fright – all systems were go and she worked at warp speed. No wonder clients loved her.

So I went back to my office and wrote a blog post for our website. It was something about how affected we can be by the odd occurrences in our lives and how it impacts our ability to be swayed by good marketing. I know it was a good point and well written. Don't ask me what I said – sometimes you just have to do it, and this was one of those times.

After writing my post I circled back to check on Kyle. I was really feeling guilty about that whole thing. He'd spoken to Garth. Garth was pretty torn up. He hadn't wanted to lose Lacy – but as his mother-in-law had pointed out – there was too much going on with his son right now for him to be selfishly involved in a relationship that would likely add to the consternation.

I had to admit the old battle-ax made sense. This poor kid had enough on his plate without being introduced to his Dad's pushy and selfish inamorata. I had to give Garth credit. He really was a good Dad. How did Claire deserve such a great guy? Another of life's mysteries. But, poor Garth was about to have the very foundation under his feet crumble.

Not to worry, Kyle assured me. Garth felt very much in control of Lacy and her angry hysterical rantings. He appreciated the heads-up, but he was not concerned. He had actually been contemplating a break with Lacy even before Claire's untimely demise. Lacy was fun but she took emotive to an art form. Garth was not sure it was something he ever wanted to expose his son to. It was hard for him. At the peak of this tempestuous relationship he had to break it off. But Garth genuinely seemed to feel it was best for both him and his son. His mother-in-law had merely echoed the concerns with which Garth was already wrestling. Poor Lacy. She was never the "love of Garth's life" as she had imagined. I made a mental note not to spend any money on that radio station for the next month or so. I hate to be mercenary but our clients' interests had to come first with me – and with half their staff running around in circles it would be a while before that station was firing on all four burners again!

[CHAPTER 37]

Back in my office I started to think about all of the different
turns this investigation was taking. Admittedly we'd come a long
way since I'd first heard of the murder from Kyle – but had we?
We'd taken facts and related insinuations and made some seemingly
logical assumptions. All of this had led us to the colossal assumption
that the murderer had been "tight" with Claire, Clovis and me.
Aside from making me chronically uneasy, I had to admit to being a
little worried. The whole team, official detectives and Marcel junior
detectives alike, were heading down a very specific road with no
clear evidence that we were pointed in the right direction.

It was so frustrating to know that we could be barking up the
wrong tree altogether. Most frustrating was the fact that there was
an above average chance that we would never truly know what had
happened to Claire. Had I been one of her friends or loved ones - hell
had I even given a damn about her - it would have driven me insane.
As it was I was invested in solving the mystery – curiosity can be
a bitch – and I really really wanted my old, safe life back. What I

wouldn't have given for a little good old boredom right about now.

I started to review all of the suspects currently at the top of the list. I had to believe that forensics had already ruled out Trixie – she just wasn't big or strong enough. My gut kept telling me that Clarke was in no way involved in this case, however I had to admit to a larger than life curiosity about his odd behavior on the automotive pitch. Maybe if I spent some time digging around about that it would take my mind off of the murder for a few blessed hours. Before launching into my side investigation, I wanted to think through the DeVille connection. That was the wild card. I didn't know Camille well at all, and from what I could see, her behavior was altered by a grand shot of "crazy" periodically.

Not being a psychoanalyst, at least not an official one, I couldn't begin to relate how the "crazy" element fit into the whole picture. Although it seemed like a stretch – I'm pretty sure throughout history "crazy" had taken many a "stretch" and turned it into a 911 emergency call, but it still didn't feel right. Then there were the threatening notes – the first one hand delivered, I was sure that woman had been nowhere near Marcel – she was too easy to spot so I would definitely have heard about it. And the second one typed out on a computer at the university library - I wasn't sure DeVille even knew we had a university in Nebraska. Sure, she could have gone in to throw us off the track – but I was guessing that this "crazy" wasn't bothering to cover any tracks. So the notes were a major stretch in relation to her.

I wasn't sure this exercise was helping anything – but it helped me get focused, so I guess that made it worthwhile. Next step, on to Clarke. I wrestled with the best means of getting to the bottom of this odd little mystery. I recall that Claire and Clovis and I had discussed Clarke's unusual behavior more than once as we worked our way through this time consuming and ultimately fruitless pitch. Oh yes, we learn from every new business experience, but the lesson is so much more gratifying when we emerge victorious! So I strained to recall the conversation we three had had concerning Clarke's odd behavior.

"I think he's in love," Clovis stated emphatically. "That always causes a man to behave erratically."

"I think you're an idiot," Claire responded deliberately, "He likes to argue, end of mystery!"

Classic Claire. Say the most shockingly, insulting thing you can think of to ensure that the person you're addressing knows the full level of disdain you have for them – and if your statement has more than one victim all the better. Clovis looked back at her with a "humph" and a pouty little girl face. I didn't disagree with Claire's assessment of Clovis and I certainly understood the temptation to share that blinding revelation with the moron, however, forcing us to withstand the pouty face was a rookie move on Claire's part. It defined the term cruel and unusual punishment.

"Thanks a lot, you smug bitch," I growled loudly.

Claire shot me a look of outright shock which immediately turned sheepish. She knew what the hell I was talking about. Conversely, Clovis turned beaming eyes on me as she mistakenly assumed that I was valiantly defending her honor. Fine, think what you want. Just try to reel in some of the drama – I'm begging you!

So we were off to our usual start.

"No, this is not Clarke's normal 'you need to be challenged on this point before we can move forward' posture. This is different," I offered thoughtfully.

"You're reading too much into the situation as usual, League," Claire countered. "This is no different from the pain in the ass he is any other day."

"There's an urgency to his arguments that is very different from the passion that I normally see," I concluded proudly.

That's what had been different. Clarke took great pride in our creative product and he was not willing to compromise. He was usually right, but not always. On those few times when we truly believed that his arguments were ill conceived we took hours to wrestle him to the ground intellectually. Of course, it's possible that we were all wrong and he was right – nevertheless that's how it went down. It always created a stimulating, albeit frustrating discussion in which the clients' best interests were well served. During these interminable discussions we examined the best solution from every angle imaginable – squared.

Being the good guy that he was, Clarke inevitably felt guilty after one of these sessions. Immediately afterward we would all share our fantasies of killing and maiming him, but in retrospect we had to admire his dedication and passion. That's what was so different about this time, it wasn't passion, it was urgency, and it was like night and day.

Clearly reviewing our past conversation was not going to give me the answer that I sought. The more I struggled with how best to move on the more it occurred to me that I should go right to the source. Clarke was about the most upfront guy I knew. Whether or not I agreed with him on an issue, I was always confident of getting an honest and forthright response from him.

I sauntered over to Clarke's office to see if he was around. As luck would have it, he was just contemplating taking a break from a particularly intense writing project. I managed to convince myself that he really was looking for a break and not just trying to be polite. I know I said he was unfailingly honest, but his slight southern drawl automatically boosted his politeness quotient to the top of the charts, so I usually felt compelled to double-check. Clarke always gave me the feeling I was conversing with a modern day cross between a cowboy and James Dean. Laid back in jeans and sneakers and tattoos, his slightly southern, gravelly- voiced delivery transported me out of the office and onto the dusty plains. Those sentences he started with the nominative pronoun magically transported me to a hot summer day where the audible sigh, after a long, cool drink, signaled blessed relief – Aaahhh know what you mean – could often be heard when passing by his doorway. Whatever the reason, my conversations with Clarke always gave me a break from the typical office hustle and bustle.

"Hey Clarke, somethin's buggin' me," I began slipping into my "yes I'm from New Jersey but I can still be a cowgirl" persona. It's not like I did it on purpose!

"Happy to help if there's anything I can do." I waited a moment for the ma'am that would have come had we actually been on the plains before moving on.

"I'll get right to the point," I offered briskly.

"Ah've kinda come to expect that," my gravelly-voiced companion drawled.

I outlined my observations as well as Claire's and Clovis's during the automotive pitch. By the time I'd finished, Clarke was sporting a discernibly different countenance. His coloring had turned from a normal skin tone to a darkish purple and then back up to a ghostly ash gray. He appeared as though he'd like to jump up from his comfortable slouch on the sofa and run. Problem was, I was blocking the door so the only way to run would have been over to and out the window. And as we were on the fourth floor that would have been a distinctly career-limiting move. Clearly I'd struck a nerve. I think even Clarke realized there was no point in equivocating – he had to have felt the bizarre chemical response that his traitorous skin had inflicted upon his best attempt at a poker face. There was no point ignoring it.

"Yeah," he offered, as he took a minute for his metabolic system to return to normal.

"Clarke," I tried to give him a few extra seconds to recoup.

"Aahh knew this one was comin' back at me sooner or later, so let's just do it," Clarke began determinedly. He was no coward.

"Okay, " I settled myself in to his visitor chair, "Lay it on me,"

"Well, Donna, "he began, "you know me and my freakishly staunch loyalties?"

I certainly did. One thing about Clarke – he was a man of honor – and nothing you could do could force him to betray a friend.

"Aahh'm not proud of this one, Donna," Clarke continued, "Well you remember that lead from the auto parts manufacturer came in through Claire, right?"

I nodded. I'd forgotten that but he was right.

"And she was all puffed up from self importance. She'd heard about it through someone from her church who was a fairly low level assistant to the head of marketing. You know how she always sucked up to those low level people at key companies – the ones she would normally humiliate for sport – but this time her sucking up seemed to pay off. This little clerical lady was so grateful for the attention Claire paid her that she called her right up when they started thinkin' about dumping their current agency. "

Yes, I was starting to remember all of that, and don't think my slow memory is menopause – we just get so much input overload that we have to jettison some things or our heads would explode. None of this had really been relevant until now with the murder investigation.

"Well, Donna, what you probably didn't know was that Claire had planned on leveraging this win into a full and equal ownership of Marcel. She'd planned on positioning herself as the one and only reason we got this business and would have exploited the situation as soon as the timing was right. In fact she'd already started planting most of the seeds with Donny, thinking he was the only owner smart enough to understand her true brilliance. In her zeal to scramble up the corporate ladder she kind of got ahead of herself. Before any of the rest of us got involved she'd already determined the strategy and creative direction for the whole pitch. And frankly, I have to admit that it wasn't half bad."

So far I'd learned some new information, but still couldn't see quite why Clarke had been so obviously uncomfortable. So I kept my mouth shut and let Clarke continue.

"We'd just about received the official RFP (request for proposal) when I got a call from an old buddy of mine from Tuscaloosa. Hadn't heard from him in years and was shocked to learn he'd moved to Nebraska. I was ready to catch up but he had other thoughts on his mind. I didn't remember him having such a mysterious side. Turned out he was workin' at the auto parts company we were pitchin.' Can you believe it? "

Clarke went on to explain that at first he thought his buddy could be a great resource, but he quickly realized that knowing this guy would prove to be nothing more than a curse. His buddy, Darryl, had told him that he'd seen the name Marcel on a list of agencies being considered and he'd remembered reading something about Clarke being at Marcel. Darryl had really agonized over whether or not to contact Clarke – but they went back too far for him to ignore the freight train that was heading straight for his buddy's place of business.

Darryl went on to explain to Clarke that our big auto parts prospect was minutes away from Chapter 11, but before filling Clarke in on the whole scenario he'd sworn him to secrecy – he was not to tell the Marcel owners any of this. Needless to say, Clarke started feeling extremely agitated. He pressed Darryl for information feeling confident that he could find a way to dissuade Liv, Donny and me from pursuing the account without revealing all of their financial woes, if he was convinced that financial disaster was imminent.

He'd also heard that Donny had already been sniffing around about their financial status – but that wasn't particularly unusual – it was just smart business. Clarke wanted some proof and Darryl was able to provide it. There were three memos from top management that spelled out everything Darryl had revealed.

Once Clarke had his proof, he felt that the path was clear. He would start with Claire. Since she was the origin of the lead and she was not an owner of Marcel, he could outline the whole situation for her. Once Claire realized the imminent danger to Marcel she could easily fabricate a reason to pull out of the pitch that would satisfy our three owners. That's where it all went wrong. Clarke confided in Claire and handed over the financial proof. He felt confident that once convinced, Claire would quickly formulate an exit strategy and we could all watch the imminent disaster from the sidelines. Far from it. She had listened intently to everything Clarke had to say. Then she'd reviewed the papers Darryl had provided to back up his story to Clarke. She finished reading and glared at Clarke.

"Okay, here's how it's going down," Claire started ominously, "You will shut the hell up and not tell your pathetic story to another soul. This Darryl is obviously a quack and he's fabricated this ridiculous crap to get us out of the running, and that's not about to happen."

"Oh, but Claire," Clarke began tenuously, "I don't…"

"Listen to me, Clarke," Claire continued with a clear threat in her voice. "Let it go."

"But how…" Normally super quick to catch on, Clarke was at a loss. He was having trouble wrapping his mind around Claire's reaction. "Claire, if there's any truth to this it could…"

"Clarke," Claire sharply interrupted him once again. "Listen to me. This is the opportunity I've been waiting for to get my rightful place in this company. If this prospect selects us, I'm in. If they fumble afterward, that can't be construed as my fault – and I'm sure a little financial upheaval won't be a blip in our own finances so what's the harm?"

"Claire," Clarke was stunned. "We just can't…"

"We can and we will, Clarke." Claire preened maliciously as she folded Darryl's papers and shoved them into her pocket. "Besides, you have no proof and you can't say anything to those three fools without breaching your precious confidence," she finished triumphantly.

Clarke went on to explain that he'd made up his mind at that point to sabotage the whole pitch. It was his only option. It explained why he and Claire had fought so bitterly throughout the whole process. For a moment I had that warm glowing feeling that all company owners get when one of their managers sticks their neck out excessively to help the company. The next moment, however, I was more perplexed than ever.

"But Clarke, the company never did go into Chapter 11," I pushed, admittedly with a bit of a whine.

"Right, Donna. Well, there are one or two more pieces of this particular puzzle," Clarke sighed. "You're correct about the company not falling apart financially, and if you recall they did the one thing that always makes agencies go nuts. They put everyone through a full pitch and then selected an agency closely connected to the people in their own company – one that they would probably have selected anyway. What they deliberately chose not to make public at the time was the fact that this agency was also closely connected by family to a "white-knight" investor firm, and the whole thing was tied up in a nice neat package to financially save the company. Luckily this opportunity presented itself just in time to keep the Chapter 11 papers from being filed. It's still uncertain as to whether enough capital has been infused to help right the ship. Just last week, I heard Donny ruminating on the fact that we may have dodged a major financial bullet based on reports he's hearing on their financial situation."

"What else?" I blurted.

"Huh?"

"You said there were one or two more things, I'm guessing that's not everything," I pushed.

"Right again, Donna, "Clarke reluctantly admitted.

He took a moment. I could tell this was going to be the most difficult part of his admission. So I waited.

"So here's the final puzzle piece," Clarke slowly revealed, "Ya know that break-in at Claire's after the murder?"

"You!" I howled.

"Yeah."

"What? Why? Oh god," I sputtered.

"I had to get Darryl's papers so they wouldn't be made public," Clarke brooded.

"So you broke into her house!" I was pretty much shrieking now.

"Yeah, well, I actually had a key, but the crime scene tape and all. Well, it just seemed like the best thing would be to get in any way I could and get the hell out before there was a full search. Once I'd broken the lock on the window I had to make it look like a robbery."

"But why the scrapbooking room?"

"You know Claire, she kept dropping these annoying little pseudo-clever hints about where she'd hidden those papers. Things like 'rest assured those papers have made it into my family history' and 'without my influence those papers would have nowhere near the colorful existence I've given them.' It didn't take a complete idiot to figure it out. So I went and got them."

"One more thing, Clarke."

"I didn't kill her, Donna."

I didn't think so.

[CHAPTER 38]

Back at my desk I quickly checked e-mails and voicemail. Oh god, the dreaded message from Clovis.

"Donna, hi. Would you mind copying all of your notes on the murder so I can review them – I'm sure you'd be reluctant to e-mail them for legal reasons and such," Clovis commanded. "I'll send Bat over on his way back from the university to pick them up".

"Bite me, Clovis," I thought. I'd have to get rid of Bat when he showed up. Shouldn't be too hard – he's easily distracted. I wasn't about to give her anything I'd put in writing. Odd though, I could have sworn I'd heard they were in one of their separated phases. Oh well, no way of keeping track of their erratic relationship – and definitely no desire!

They had the weirdest and creepiest relationship any of us had ever encountered. When they were together she was either "over the moon" in love and telling all of us that he was constantly fending off offers of high paying, huge visibility jobs from the most elite of the Fortune 1,000. He was gorgeous, he was brilliant, everyone loved him, blah, blah, blah – or – he was her little flunky, running around to do her bidding. Guess I knew where they stood now.

When they were separated it was considerably different. She painted a picture of him as controlling and emotionally abusive. His emotional abuse would rapidly evolve into physical abuse when provoked, and let's face it, Clovis could provoke a saint. She painted the picture of a monster who should not be allowed on the street – much less in her bed. From our contact with both Clovis and Bat we'd drawn few absolute conclusions. We really didn't know truth from fiction in her ever-changing monologues. One thing we did know was that Bat was creepy. We all felt it.

When they were "on" Bat tried really hard to be all the things that Clovis envisioned, and in truth he could be very charming in a dark and disturbing sort of way. Maybe he appealed to the dark side in all of us. Though we all tried to suppress it and treat him with the bored indifference that his borderline comical presence in our world warranted, I think he genuinely thrived on that barely detectable shudder that none of us could ever successfully repress upon his entrance into a room.

Once I had finished putting out the typical garden variety fires that tended to pop up daily, I took a minute to contemplate any incomplete action steps that might require my attention. For the first time in the investigation I couldn't think of any identified gaps in our knowledge that I'd be able to fill. Sure, there were still some unanswered questions but most of them had been rigorously examined by the police and/or the coroner's office. Odds of my miraculously coming up with those answers were slim to none. That whole murder weapon mystery was proving to be quite a puzzle.

So I took another tack. Were there any questions that jumped to mind? Facts that were there but hadn't really garnered much attention? As I ran through the various pieces of the puzzle I was hard pressed to find something that hadn't been explored fairly thoroughly. One thought did occur to me, though. Early on we had learned that Claire and Garth were having some work done to their house, hence our little but eventful road trip to their digs. It struck me as odd that I didn't remember hearing it had come up in any of Kyle's conversations with Garth. It was probably another dead end – but I felt the need to make a useful contribution at this juncture. Eliminating yet another possibility would qualify.

I made a few phone calls and found that the work was being done by a builder out of Plattsmouth. That seemed odd. Why not choose one of the many builders within the Omaha city limits? I walked to the next office to let my police escort know that I'd be embarking on a brief road trip, and then I walked over to "creative" to find Babs and Peg. I can't tell you why, but I always felt safer when they were along. Let's not even contemplate what that says about me! After a ten minute lecture in which I forced Babs to swear that she would never under any circumstances involve me in what could in any way be construed as ridiculous and embarrassing behavior, we were ready to set out for Plattsmouth.

My security detail was exuberant because I'd promised to take them to one of Plattsmouth's finest eating establishments for an early lunch. Babs and Peg were elated. They lived for adventure, and this past week had been a dream come true. I was uncharacteristically quiet on the trip as I pondered what the hell I would say to this builder and how on earth this could possibly be relevant to the case. Second thoughts can be a bitch!

We found the sad dumpy looking little construction building in a quarry-like setting near the edge of town. Where the hell did Claire find this company? It looked pretty deserted but an elderly woman was sitting at the lone desk inside and she seemed willing to chat. She told us that the owner, Ben, was on a job site and would probably not return until after lunch. She was aware that they'd been doing a residential in Omaha but didn't seem to know many details. Betty, as we later found out, was Ben's aunt and his office help. Aunt Betty told us Ben was focusing on jobs close to home base this month, and we were not to assume that this building we stood in was representative of her nephew's work product. In fact this month they were scheduled to spend a little time putting his office building back into shape. Ben had recently inherited it from another branch of the family and he just hadn't had the chance to make any of the badly needed repairs. I have to admit, when I saw the state of Ben's office building I had the briefest inkling that Claire had taken leave of her senses at some point prior to her murder. Who the hell would hire this guy to reconstruct their house?

Betty then suggested that we head on over to the local grill house for lunch. Don't ask me why in a tiny little town like Plattsmouth there is a renowned and heralded eatery. Seems odd to me – but what do I know. I'm from New Jersey! Well, at least that's where I started out. Betty felt that we'd stand a good chance of running into Ben there since that was his preferred dining choice when working on local jobs.

Riley and O'Dowd knew their way around Plattsmouth, so finding the place was a breeze. They managed to grab the one empty table. It was a tad small for five diners but beggars can't be choosers. Although extremely small, it was the largest and most solid looking table in the place. As I glanced around it was hard to ignore the fact that the walls were raw lumber sans sheet rock or insulation and the handful of tables were crammed together in a fashion that would have deterred even the mildest of claustrophobics from ever walking through the door. The two small windows were tinged with filth and the heat of the oven could be felt throughout. Observing the many faces, mostly male, crowded around those rickety tables told a story of contented bliss. We'd heard the food was legendary and apparently we hadn't heard wrong.

We asked our server if Ben Caswell was there. Ben sat in the corner with a bunch of guys that looked like construction workers. They were all chowing down on some heavenly smelling stew. Whether or not this trip made any headway in solving the murder – I was definitely having that stew!

We let the guys finish their lunch and had about finished our own when we saw Ben rise to leave. He appeared to be a fairly average looking contractor-type guy, not too tall, or heavy, not all that hairy, but he was clad in the prerequisite jeans, work boots and t-shirt with the odd tool hanging out here or there. Some of them looked like they might hurt if he sat on them wrong.

Riley yelled over to him, "You Caswell?"

"Whattya need?" he grumbled in return.

"Gotta coupla questions," Riley continued.

"Gotta check in with the office right now," he informed us, "It's pretty close – we can talk there."

"Aunt Betty?" I inquired knowingly.

Ben blushed, "Yeah," he responded sheepishly.

Back at Ben's office it suddenly seemed to occur to him that, including Aunt Betty, there were seven of us. We'd be hard pressed to cram five into that tiny hovel without fear of permanently damaging anyone's spleen in the process. So Ben haltingly suggested that at least two of us consider waiting in the car. "Uh, we're gonna expand when we renovate in a few weeks, " he offered weakly. Tough to feel like a big-shot builder with this fright of a building to represent your business. I thought this renovation could happen none too quickly. Little did I know how prophetic my thought would be.

O'Dowd shot a look at Babs and Peg who were marching determinedly into the itty bitty building. "Ladies," he began in a marginally sweet tone, "We're not going to be outside while Donna is in the building."

"You don't think we're..." Peg began.

"Yes, officers, Peg and I will be happy to wait outside," Babs overrode Peg's objections.

Well, it only made sense. The five of us convened in the new and soon to be renewed home of Caswell Construction. We explained to Ben that none of us seemed to have a handle on this construction project that was currently underway at the Dockens residence.

"Yeah," Ben began, "Damndest thing her gettin' killed like that.

And I hate to sound like a cantankerous old mule, but they damn well got my equipment all tied up in knots fer evidence. I kinda need that stuff. I'm not all that well fixed fer money, as you've probably already guessed."

Yes, we could see that Ben's was a business in its infancy. Any setbacks such as the temporary loss of valuable equipment could prove incredibly problematic. I felt bad for him. But I was starting to get increasingly curious about this renovation he'd been handling for Claire.

"Ben, not to sound rude," I offered. It is my contention that you can say whatever you want as long as you preface it with "Not to sound...." Obviously I was about to say something extremely rude. Anyone would know that. "Why would Claire hire such an inexperienced firm for reconstruction on her house?"

"That's a mighty good question Ms. Leigh," Ben responded unabashedly, "I've kinda been askin' myself that lately. I mean, at first I was excited as a beaver in a lumber camp. Gettin' a big residential job like that sure got me to thinkin' all my dreamin' was startin' to pay off. Mosta our jobs are replacin' missin' bricks in a wall or somethin.'

More we got into the job, I got to suspectin' that her reason for choosin' us was more 'bout wantin' someone desprit enough fer cash to suffer workin' with a danged stone crazy she-devil. 'Cause that's sure is what she was, may the lord rest her soul. We didn't do nothin' right from the get go. Fact is, I had a mind to pull my boys outta that hornets' nest and move on down the road, 'til we heard..., well, you know . "

"So you hated Claire," I stated bluntly.

"Well, ya know, ma'am, not enough ta send'er to her great reward in the sky, if that's what yer thinkin'. 'Sides, there was somethin' got us through even her screamin' howler monkey days; knowin' her ole man, Mr. Garth. He was a real nice feller. Mr. Garth was always goin' around apologizin' fer somethin' after he knew fer a fact Ms. Claire was headed out for a spell. Lotta days he didn't have a rooster's notion in a empty henhouse about what had got her to gripin', but he took to apologizin' 'cause he knew, with her, there was 'most always some bee in that bonnet . That was one hombre who sure as shoot knew his woman."

I had to force myself to focus. It happens every time someone "ma'ams" me. Don't they know that women my age would rather be called almost anything but ma'am? Even the dreaded "lady" is preferable to ma'am's ,"I must acknowledge that I'm speaking to an old woman" message. Okay girl, get your act together and concentrate on the witness!

Ben went on to say, "Truth is, Mr. Garth's the only reason we stuck it out so long. We felt real sorry for him. He tried real hard but she never failed ta see the dark rain clouds rollin' in over the parade, even when a blind man could see the sun burnin' so bright it was like to fricassee yer scalp. Fact is, we probly woulda stayed and finished the job for Mr. Garth. Hell, we'd already got more'n halfway through anyway.

I think I kin say fer sure, though. No need fer cash would make me durn fool enough to git close to that rattlesnake agin – lord bless her soul. I was just happy that I'd probly get out alive – I wuddin' sure about Mr. Garth though – that guy sure seemed like a goner. Heard somethin' about them gettin' divorced – woulda been the smartest move he coulda made. Oh shoot, you don't think he killed his ole lady do ya?"

"We're not really at liberty to reveal details of the investigation, Sir," responded Riley. "Although at this time our list of suspects is fairly extensive."

"Oh sure, hell, what wuz I thinkin'," Ben replied apologetically. "I watch Law n'Order, I shoulda knowd you couldn't answer them kinda questions – mighty sorry 'bout that."

"No sweat, Buddy," Riley replied, "It's natural to be curious."

"Well," I continued, anxious to get to the point of this whole road trip. "Why were they doing this renovation anyway?: Do you know, Ben?"

"Sure," he countered readily. "Least-wise I know what she told me," he corrected.

"What did Claire tell you, Ben?" I urged.

"Said she'd be comin' into some money real soon. Said her big fancy job was fixin' to get fancier and she'd be needin' her house to commence to bein', like she kept on tellin' us,"suitable to her position"," he stated matter-of-factly.

Oh god, she was a piece of work. I groaned inwardly. Who is that full of themselves? Well, I shouldn't wonder, I certainly knew her well enough to be convinced Ben was being genuinely candid and in no way exaggerating his response. Just as I was beginning to formulate a follow-up question, I heard a loud groaning noise and could swear that the lights flickered slightly, and was it my imagination or had one or two of the pictures on the wall shifted? Holy shit, it had to be an earthquake. Simultaneously, Ben, Riley, Aunt Betty, O'Dowd and I shot each other looks ranging from serious concern to outright terror (that would be me) as we nearly pummeled each other racing outside to safety.

Once outside the groaning evolved into grinding and gnashing and the movement was still vaguely evident. Just as two key points occurred to me: One, I didn't see Babs and Peg, and two, the ground was not shaking – only the building. A hideous, inhuman screeching noise accompanied by a serious swaying of the building resulting in puffs of thick bilious dust were followed by an enormous crash as we all stood with our mouths hanging open and watched the building in which we'd just had our tete-a-tete come tumbling down. In the midst of the wreckage, behind the fallen ruins of the Caswell Construction home office stood Babs and Peg – Babs clutching a two by four with both hands.

In a million years I could not have imagined that even Babs and Peg could be capable of this kind of devastation – I was speechless. Peg was the first to regain her composure.

"Hey guys, it's not what you think," she began.

As the voluminous dust settled over all of our clothes and our hair, in our eyes and mouths, I had only one comment.

"Really? I think Babs grabbed a two by four attached to the building and the building fell down."

"Well, yeah, that is what happened," Peg acknowledged diligently, "But…"

"Well it was, y'know, it was leaning. And it looked kind of

unstable." Babs found her voice, "So I just kinda thought I'd help out and straighten it up, y'know, to be more stable."

As a heavy cloud of dust covered Ben's ghost white face I began to hear what sounded like a keening noise coming from his general direction. This low eerie sound began to build until it reached a reverberating groan ending in a growl. We looked at Ben. He didn't look good. Aunt Betty ran over – after wiping the majority of the soot out of her eyes – and grabbed his arm fearing that he was about to keel over.

It took about 45 minutes before Ben finally seemed to come around. We had seriously debated calling 911, but it's not like the building had fallen on him or anything. Besides, my bodyguards were well-versed in the treatment of shock. They ministered to Ben for a bit, accompanied by vehement orders from Aunt Betty. Once Ben was somewhat back to normal, he looked to Babs. We motioned for her to step toward him and she sheepishly complied.

"Oh Ben, I am so sorry…" Babs apologized.

"No Babs," Ben offered guiltily. "In fact I think you coulda actually did me a mighty big favor. Now I reccon' we'll be gettin' a big ole insurance check so we kin rebuild our buildin' better'n ever. That money'll sure come in handy right about now.

I hafta admit seein' the office come tumblin' down like that hit me like a sucker punch to the gut. Not 'cause it was you moved the board'n made it fall – but 'cause the dang thing was a far sight worse than I'd reconned. How'd I miss seein' that? We were just plum stupid to think that puny board could keep the whole thing from cavin' in. We'da never let people into the blamed thing if we'da knowd how bad it had got. Truth be told, Babs, you're kind of a hero 'cause I think you just mighta saved Aunt Betty's life. I'm powerful grateful to ya fer that! My Mom will be too."

Babs' face went from abject sorrow and humiliation to triumphant jubilation in less than a minute. To an observer it was absolutely fascinating.

"Well Ben, I'm happy to help anytime," was Babs' retort.

Unbelievable.

[CHAPTER 39]

Bing. We got off the elevator and you guessed it. Donny was there to greet us.

"Hey Donna, Kirby called from building maintenance, they're thinking about knocking this building down and they'd like to hire you for a consult. I told him that our price per hour for demolition is a lot higher than branding. Hell, we've got to cover those high insurance premiums. I think I can honestly say that I've never been happier!"

"Y'know Donny," I began forcefully.

"No, don't Donna, I want to remember this moment just as it is – don't spoil it."

"Humph," Was the best I could do as I ushered my girls into another part of the building. Donny and his homeboys headed over to his office, I was sure, to relive our most recent adventure. Fine. I might be a destructive and unstoppable force, but at least I didn't have to live vicariously through my partner – so there! As the boys moved toward the creative living room, Riley turned back to remind me.

"Hey Donna, don't forget you're flying solo for a few hours while we go back to the station for a recap meeting."

I guess the task force had decided that I wasn't as much at risk as they'd originally feared, because it definitely seemed as though my protection was not as high on their list after just a short time without another threatening note. I had to admit, though, that it was kind of a relief not to have those two gorillas so close all the time. After all it was only a few hours. They would be back mid-evening and I knew there'd be a patrol on my house overnight.

I dropped Babs and Peg off in "creative" where they were deluged with questions about the day's activities. When I left them they were every bit the conquering heroes that could leap – or eradicate – tall buildings in a single bound. God bless them.

I went in search of Kyle and found that he had a meeting at our healthcare client. Apparently he'd been there since late morning, and word was that he might still be there for dinner. Clearly that was a dead end, and I so wanted to see if he'd learned anything new today. Oh well, I'd just have to wait. Not my best thing – maybe he'd call after his meeting – I could only hope.

I checked messages and found a cryptic one from Tina.

"Hey Donna," she chirped, "Give me a buzz when you get a minute. I've got some new info on the victim and our erstwhile insurance putz. I really don't think it's anything, but it might make you laugh. Talk to you later."

I made a note to buzz Tina before leaving for home that night, but first I had to tackle the expense accounts or there'd be a revolution for sure. They say the only things that are certain are death and taxes – they forgot the volatile reaction caused by late expense checks.

I walked around the agency and talked to a few of the staff members, checking on the agency capabilities pieces (our boilerplate promotional materials) and the new video for our website. Things were moving along so I figured I'd make my call to Tina and head on home for the night. From the looks of things, Riley and O'Dowd had already left for the station.

When I got back to my office there was an e-mail from Kyle. "I'm on a quick break and the meeting's almost over. I need you to meet me in the parking lot of the Holiday Inn – the murder site – at 6 pm. I want to meet at six to be sure that I'll get there ahead of you – I don't want you waiting in that parking lot alone. Don't worry, I just want to show you something and then we'll go right over to the FarmHouse for a quick salad and an update. I've asked your safety patrol to meet us there so that they can escort you home."

Oh good. I was really hoping to get a chance to catch up with Kyle tonight. That seemed like a perfect suggestion and he was right – hell could freeze over before I'd consider waiting in that parking lot alone. I'd feel safer having Riley and O'Dowd escort me home. I had to admit I was a bit curious as to what Kyle wanted me to see, well actually, more excited than curious. It had to be good or he'd never have suggested my driving over there. With our upcoming meeting and some important information to look forward to, I tried to concentrate on writing one last blog post for the Marcel website before heading out. Knowing that focus would be an issue I settled for writing some short but valuable "tips" on writing blogs.

By the time I looked up it was 5:50. Oh shit, I don't want to leave Kyle waiting. I packed up my stuff and entered my time – didn't want to get locked out of the computer in the morning. I thought about calling Kyle to let him know I was on my way but I knew I'd lose my signal in the elevator. Once I got into my car I figured there was really no point since the traffic had waned and I'd make it there by five after six at the latest.

[CHAPTER 40]

When I got to the Holiday Inn parking lot it was darker than I'd expected. The crime scene was cleared away but you could still tell that something had occurred there. I have to admit it gave me a chill. I looked around the parking lot for Kyle's SUV. Wow, that was a surprise. All that rushing and it appeared as though I'd beaten him over here - figures. I wasn't sure I was at all thrilled about that. I figured I'd drive around the perimeter of the lot for a few minutes before looking for a place to park. I didn't want to be any closer to the scene of the crime than I had to be. After about five more minutes I was starting to get impatient. You can never really control these client meetings, so when they end is often a complete surprise. Better not call Kyle, though, if they were wrapping up he'd have his phone off anyway.

I was getting sick of circling the parking lot so I decided to park near the most well-lit doorway. There was some kind of a dinner on the other side of the building so that's where I headed. I parked my car and headed into the well-lit banquet hall. Once inside I realized that I was among longhorn cattle ranchers. Why not? They're as good a group as any, and I was damned if I was gonna be alone in the dark.

I spent another ten minutes or so walking among the ranchers. It was starting to get on my nerves. I figured that, at this point, Kyle would have told the client that he was late for another meeting and excused himself. Of course, he'd be here any moment. Why not take this opportunity to visit the ladies' room. That way we could get right down to business when he got here. I decided to bypass the rancher ladies' restroom in favor of the next one down the hallway. I did have to walk through an area that was not well-lit but I found the restroom and ducked inside. When I hit the light switch my heart almost stopped. There in the middle of the ladies' room was Bat holding tightly to a large, lumpy looking duffel bag. Holy Mother of God if that didn't give me a heart attack I sure as crap don't know what would.

"Bat, for god's sake what the hell are you doing here?" I bellowed.

"Hi Donna, good to see you," he replied softly.

"Bat, Bat you didn't answer my question, what the hell are you doing here?" I pushed harder.

"Oh Donna, I'm really glad to see you. I have some things that are bothering me and I could really use someone to talk to. You always seem like such a well-balanced person." Bat continued, as if he could actually recognize a well-balanced person if he saw one.

"Well, Bat," I replied with more confidence.

How very perceptive of Bat, I thought. He'd made an excellent point I WAS always very helpful to those with difficult to resolve issues – maybe I hadn't been giving him enough credit. Maybe I'd actually have to like the guy.

"Uh, Donna?" he mumbled.

"Oh right, Bat," I continued "I'd love to help you out in any way I can, but I'm supposed to be meeting Kyle out near the entrance momentarily." I looked around the large, newly renovated ladies' room with its insipid beige tile as far as the eye could see. Bat and I stood at opposite corners of the enclosure like opponents in a fighting ring. To my dismay, Bat stood closer to the only exit door. That was unfortunate.

I suddenly realized Bat was talking again.

"Oh yeah, okay, well maybe you could talk to me until he gets here?" he replied somewhat sheepishly.

"Sure what the hell, he's obviously more tied up than he'd expected. We'll just have to be on the watch for him," I reasoned.

"Yeah Donna, that would be good," he eagerly countered.

"Okay Bat, so what's bothering you?" I started, wondering how much I'd regret this decision.

"Well, Donna, you know that Clovis and I have had our problems," he offered.

I think that may have been the understatement of the century. Clovis and Bat had had their problems? Clovis and Bat were a freakin' train wreck. Bonnie and Clyde had had their problems. Clovis and Bat made them look like lightweights.

"Yes, I think I've heard something about that, Bat." I tried to sound convincing but I had to bite my lip hard to keep from guffawing out loud. "But I don't really know any of the details of what you two have been through, I try not to nose around in other people's lives," I finished, blushing furiously. I'd never been very good at lying. Luckily, Bat was too self-involved to notice my obvious discomfort.

"Really Donna?" Bat queried. "But aren't you the lead detective on this murder investigation?"

"No Bat. Where on earth did you get that? How would I be a lead detective in anything? I'm not even a detective. No Bat. At best I'm an amateur sleuth who hasn't discovered one piece of solid evidence in this whole mess." I was starting to resent Bat for making me see myself in a decidedly less than flattering light. Jackass. Why did he have to push this anyway? Why do I waste time on morons?

"Oh, Donna, that's not what people think," countered Bat gently.

"What are you talking about Bat? What people?" I fairly screeched. This was really getting annoying. How did he get away from his keeper anyway?

"Well, Clovis for one." Bat offered sweetly.

Just great. How do you tell the decidedly off balance on-again, off-again boyfriend of a genuinely certifiable complete and utterly insane lunatic nutjob card-carrying kook that she's not the most reliable source that's ever lived. I was at a bit of an impasse.

"Well Bat, it seems Clovis has her facts wrong for once," I ad-libbed questionably. "I'm a little reluctant to involve myself in your private relationship with Clovis in any case. It just seems like too much of an invasion of your privacy or something. Besides, I can't imagine that there's anything I could do…"

"Oh Donna, don't be so modest." Bat countered, "I've seen how good you are with people in need of comfort. Like Peg when she trashed that cop car, or Babs after she knocked that building down. You have a real knack for seeing the truth and making people feel better about pretty much anything."

Now I really was starting to blush, and feeling that Bat was really much brighter than anyone'd given him credit for in the past. Yes, he was actually fairly intelligent. Why I.....wait a second! How the hell did Bat know about all of those things? I shot him a "look" – half quizzical and half creeped out. Based on his next comment my "looks" hadn't lost any of their power.

"That damn Clovis. She was so worried about this whole investigation and she started cryin' that she was the lead suspect, so I promised her I'd nose around and find out what was goin' on. Since she assumed that you were the center of it all, Donna, she's been pretty much havin' me tail you for the past week or so. She wanted to know your every move."

What?!?!?! I was kind of in shock, and I was definitely creeped out. My radar was on full bore. The thought of Bat watching my every move was about to cause a seismic shudder in my system that had little hope of being controlled anytime in this decade. I had to get control of myself before Bat saw my consternation. If he was enough of a nut job to be following me around, I really didn't want to upset his mental applecart any further than necessary. I took a few deep breaths and tried to think of what I could possibly say after his incredibly damning and oh-so-disturbing admission.

"Bat, I'm going to have to see if Kyle is here yet." I had nothing –

still shaken to the core - I had to fall back on repeating myself. It was amazing how incredibly disorienting it was to discover that you were being followed. And it didn't help that it was the creepy boyfriend of the office lunatic –sorry, make that former office lunatic.

"About that, Donna." Bat replied hesitantly.

I looked at him. He swallowed hard.

"Kyle's not coming," Bat spit out.

"What, did you talk to him? How do you know?" I responded trying to keep my voice from sounding too frantic.

"He was never coming, Donna," Bat finished solemnly.

My head was spinning. I had to sit down.

"I, I don't understand. I got an e-mail…" I stammered.

"No Donna, that was from me," Bat admitted.

"No Bat, it was sent from Kyle's computer," I argued.

"Yes, Donna. I sent it from Kyle's computer," he declared calmly.

That's when it hit me. I knew where the threatening notes had come from. Now I had to ask myself – was I standing here talking to Claire's killer? My guess was, yes.

"But Bat," I queried gently, "How could you possibly know that I would come into this ladies' room?"

"It was a chance I had to take, Donna," he retorted, "I couldn't very well hide out in the overcrowded 'steer ladies' rest room now could I? Besides, I know your dislike of crowded areas so I figured you'd wind your way down here at some point. And I have loads of patience. The fact remains, I just had to talk to you!"

Hmmph, maybe this guy's not quite as dumb as I'd thought. No, I was pretty sure he was.

I gulped a few times. Then I took a few more deep breaths. I needed to think. But there was no time. In the scheme of things I figured I had one thing going for me. Bat didn't seem dangerous. At least not any more than he ever did – and that was more attention getting instability than raw danger. I needed time to think and I was in a position to buy some time. Bat didn't know of my suspicions. He merely knew that I was confused as to why he'd send me an e-mail from Kyle's computer. I'd have to play along – keep him talking, and above all keep him calm.

If he did murder Claire and it was an emotional act – I had to keep this an emotionless conversation. I had no idea what I could possibly do to save myself if he was the murderer – but I could keep the conversation going indefinitely. Actually, that's kind of one of my specialties. I have won many a negotiation because I talked the other party into exhaustion and finally submission. This time I'd be talking to save my life.

It was critical that I not let Bat touch on any incendiary issues. Steer clear of the murder and his real reason for tricking me into coming here. I could only imagine what that was. I'd have to pretend that I was really concerned over his relationship with Clovis and I really wanted to help. Man that was gonna be a tough one – lifesaving or not. Well, it was clear what had to be done and there was no time like the present.

"Bat, what difference does it make how we got here? You're clearly in pain and I think I can probably help," I urged. "Why don't you tell me about you and Clovis." Urp, oh god, heartburn – and that felt like a mini throw-up in my mouth. I don't know if it was from

245

fear or because that was a tough sentence to get out. Luckily Bat was no rocket scientist.

"I guess," Bat eased into his favorite topic, "I just don't get that woman, Donna. Why does she mess me up like this?"

Oh man, where do I go with this? Don't start picking on Bat or you'll piss him off. Don't start picking on Clovis or you might piss him off more. Okay, here goes – we're talkin' full out romantic fantasy. In other words I was gonna lie my ass off! Man, I hoped he was as dumb as I thought he was.

"Well Bat, there's one thing I know for sure," I began hopefully. "You and Clovis are meant to be together. You will work out your problems and be together forever."

"Forever in hell!" I was thinking.

"That is something I know in my heart, dear Bat," I continued trying hard not to gag.

Oh shit, I sounded just like a Tammy Wynette song – and I don't even like country. I was making myself sick. Even an idiot would realize that I didn't have a sincere bone in my body. What made things even worse was that I was starting to get really nervous, so I was sweating – a lot – and I could feel my face starting to turn red. Really menopause – NOW you have to start with the symptoms?

"Oh Donna, do you really think so?" Bat cooed. "Well I know you do, I can tell by how emotional you're getting about everything. Donna, you are such a good friend to Clovis and me. How can we ever thank you?"

The asshole bought it. Holy crap! I AM good! I rocked that big ass lie! That's right, I can't be stopped!!! Okay, time for another round – let's see how far I can take it this time. And dial it down girlfriend before you get yourself – never mind – won't even voice that in my head.

"You know, Bat, Clovis has told me many times that you are the love of her life and that she can't imagine living without you," I breezed out.

"Oh yeah?" Bat barked angrily.

Oh god, we don't want anger here – gotta get him back into tranquility mode – don't want to get him riled up about anything right about now – crap! – where did I go wrong? It was going so well!

"If she's so crazy about me, why is she always breakin' up with me? And why is she always driving me crazy with all her moods and nutty ideas?"

"Oh Bat," I began confidently.

I was treading water and the sharks were circling, but I couldn't let him see me sweat. Amazing what we're capable of doing when our life depends on it!

"She breaks up with you because she's afraid she's not good enough for you and she's afraid you'll realize that and want to leave her forever. You know she has huge self-confidence issues, always has – stems from childhood when her gypsy family was unwanted in many areas of the country."

Damn, I am good. Let's just hope he buys it.

"You really are something, Donna," Bat sounded cheerier. "Of course you're right. I can't believe I couldn't see that on my own. You're very good at this aren't you?"

Whew. I would live for yet a few more minutes. This was the closest I'd ever come to fighting for my life. And my secret weapon was my ability to sling shit that a toddler could see through and make this idiot believe it like gospel. I was feeling very grateful for low IQs right about then. But careful, don't get lulled into a false sense of security. Stay alert.

"So, now why do you think she drives me crazy with her moods, Donna?" Bat whined.

Oh god, maybe it would have been better if he'd shot me. I'm quite sure it would have been less painful.

"Well Bat," I drew out my answer as I mentally floundered to think of something to say, "I know she's always trying to make you jealous so she can test your love for her. That can certainly make a man crazy. But you know you should really be flattered that she cares so much for you she has to keep testing your love for her."

Oh man, this time I'm sure I've gone too far. That might have been the dumbest thing I've ever said. It doesn't even make sense. He's going to kill me right here in this ladies' room, and I really can't blame him. If someone said that to me I'd certainly feel justified in killing them.

"Donna, how can I ever thank you?" Bat purred.

Maybe I would find something heavy and hit him on the head. I didn't see how I'd be able to live with myself after having this conversation anyway. The memory would haunt me for years. Stop flattering yourself and think of something else to say to the moron. Buy more time! As I prepared to go on I began to search frantically for anything lying around that could be used as a weapon. I mean we couldn't go on like this indefinitely. There were slim pickins' in that ladies' room.

That was when I noticed that Bat had brought a duffel bag with him. I wondered if there was anything hard enough to use as a weapon, or if I could get close enough to grab it. Too much risk, better keep talking. Just as I was about to reenter the glamorous world of Clovis and Bat he changed the subject.

"Donna, I tricked you into coming here for another reason," Bat admitted sheepishly, "There's something I need to tell you."

Oh god no, this couldn't be good. Try to change the subject back – fast!

"Look, Bat, it's clear you're under a great deal of stress. I think we can agree that we should focus on your relationship with Clovis, get that back on track. Then you'll see, all will be right with the world." I tap danced verbally in a desperate attempt to keep Bat from revealing anything that could not be unrevealed. Once he confessed I'd be a dead woman!

"No Donna, I need to get this out. It's been eating at me and I can't take it anymore." Bat resumed sadly.

"Well hell, Bat." I continued desperately, "No need to confide any secrets to me. I mean, like I said, I haven't really been all that involved in this whole investigation."

"Donna, I killed her," Bat confessed.

This time my heart really did stop beating – for at least five minutes. Well, it seemed like that anyway. I was frozen, and terrified. I knew what this meant. There was no way Bat was going to let me live after this. I started to think about Jon and my beautiful bulldogs. I would never see any of them again. Why, oh why me? True to form my brain started working again. Was there any way that I could use this and buy some more time. I had to think of something and now I was pretty sure that there would be a hard object in that duffel bag. Could I distract him enough to grab it and turn it on him? I had to give it my best shot.

"Listen, Bat, I really don't want to get involved in this," I started indignantly. "I hated Claire and I'm not sorry she's dead. I could never be a hypocrite and turn on her murderer. Hell, you're my new hero. We should go to the bar and I'll buy you a drink for ridding the world of one of its true evils."

"Don't Donna," Bat continued.

Really? He's gonna turn Boy Scout now? I thought nervously.

"I'll admit I lured you here to kill you so that you wouldn't find the truth," he continued.

Okay, this was NOT making me feel any better – whatsoever!

"But now that we're here I realize that I need to tell you everything. I need to," Bat urged.

"All right Bat," I replied dejectedly. I knew when it was time to shut up and let someone else talk.

"Claire was using Clovis," he began. "She was trying to get Clovis to lure her husband, Garth, away from that other woman. Not because she loved him or wanted to work it out with him – just to spite him. And you know Clovis, always lookin' for an opportunity to prove that another man is hot for her. I don't mind sayin' I was pretty pissed about the whole thing. I mean you know, Donna, how that woman loved to toy with other people's lives like they were worthless garbage. I'd called Claire earlier in the day and told her we had to talk about the whole thing. She asked me to meet her in a particular spot after the Boy Scout dinner had let out. She even had me show up near the end of the dinner so she could point out the exact location. It was a spot right near the front of the building. I realized later she was hopin' someone'd seen us and would tell Clovis.

"Later that night my buddy dropped me off in the parking lot. I'd been workin' on some carburetor problems on my new motorcycle so I had some of the parts in my duffel bag here. I saw Claire's car parked in the exact spot she'd indicated so I walked over to try and talk some sense into her. I started to tell her she needed to back off on this whole scheme with Garth and Clovis. Donna, she looked at me and laughed."

Here Bat took a moment to compose himself. Poor guy, everyone who'd ever had contact with Claire knew of all her little humiliating games and forms of torture for everyone around her. This was his first exposure – and it hit him right where he lived. I actually felt sorry for him. Not sorry enough to keep from strategizing as to how I could get my hands on that damn duffel bag. I felt the need to say something at this point.

"I'm sorry, Bat," I added lamely. "Not surprised, but very sorry."

"Thanks Donna, I know you are," he added gratefully. "That's when she told me the rest of her plan."

Oh god, Claire and her intricate plans to manipulate everyone. This time it finally got her killed – but unfortunately it was probably about to get me killed as well.

"Yeah Donna, she said that she appreciated my showing up. She'd already started planting the seed with Clovis that she had a date later that night. She was going to tell Clovis that she and I were having an affair to spur Clovis into the arms of Garth and destroy his happiness forever."

Man, that would sure destroy anyone's happiness. Sure fire. Bat went on.

"I just lost it, Donna," Bat resumed his sad tale. "She kept on laughing and then she turned her back on me. She said "Get lost, you pathetic loser. You're too stupid to try and beat me." And I reached for the first convenient thing. I hoisted my duffel bag in a fit of rage and conked her right in the back of her head. When I realized what I'd done I could see that this piece of my tailpipe cut like a spawning salmon –I do love to go salmon fishing – had really made a mess of her skull.

"I don't remember anything else except that once I realized what I'd done I ran into the Holiday Inn to find some deserted work boots. I figured I could throw the cops off my scent. I took the boots and rubbed them in some nearby mud and made footprints near her body and her car. I even threw a bunch of mud on her feet so they'd think the actual murder was committed somewhere else."

Of course, I should have known that Claire would never permit mud to touch her precious designer shoes, how did I not see that before?

"I was desperate - I was afraid I'd never get to be with Clovis again. Donna can you help me?"

Okay, let's review. I have been lured into this deserted Holiday

Inn bathroom to be killed. Instead of being killed - yet - I get to play the role of armchair psychiatrist and mother confessor. I just about recover from the shock of finding crazy Bat in the darkened ladies' room, where he actually admits his plan was to bump me off – more shock. Now for the final shocker – I'm standing all alone with Claire's killer, and my stalker, who is coincidentally holding the murder weapon, and his biggest concern is NOT the electric chair looming in his immediate future but rather whether or not he'll get to date his girlfriend again. With virtually no time to process all of this, my only goal here is to search for a line of conversation that will keep him from reaching into his little bag of tricks and applying said murder weapon to my skull, thus making me the second notch on his tailpipe. At least I'm assuming I would be second – perhaps I'm being hasty in that assumption. At this point I had to realize that anything was possible. So I took a shot.

"Oh, Bat you poor thing. I had no idea you'd been through all of this," I ventured. "Of course I'll do anything I can to help you. In fact, I have a few ideas already – nothing elaborate at this point – but I think you'll be just fine."

Okay, maybe I went too far here.

"Donna, I really want to trust you here," Bat choked out hesitantly, "but I just don't know."

This was definitely not good. I had to win his trust or get my hands on that salmon-shaped pipe, the one that makes odd-shaped murder wounds, and no damn time to think things through. Time to pull out the old negotiating tools and pray.

"You're right Bat," I replied aggressively. "There is absolutely no reason for you to trust me. Why you hardly know me. If I were you, I wouldn't trust me at all."

Pray, pray and then pray some more. It always worked with sales reps – but a lot of them were more stable than Bat. Just keep praying.

"Oh no, Donna," Bat quickly reassured me. "I think there are many reasons to trust you. It's just that…"

Whew!!! It was working. Now just stay the course for a while.

"Really Bat?" I gave it my best southern-belle-without-the-accent swoop, "Do you really feel as though you can trust me? You don't know what that means to me."

Don't go too far here – this is the big curve in that Indy race. Too much gas and you flip right over – not enough and there's no chance of winning, and not winning was not an option here.

"Oh sure, Donna," Bat continued hesitantly. "I don't know what I was thinkin.' I'm just so confused, and I feel so alone."

Bring it home to Mama, that's right. Just as I was about to reply I thought I heard a little squeak. Forget that. Just press on. Too much depends on this.

"I can imagine, Bat," I sympathized.

There was that noise again. Did we have company?

"You know Bat," I continued…

At that moment the noise got much louder and the bathroom door crashed inward. There in all his superhero glory, stood Kyle.

"What the hell is going on in here?" Kyle demanded.

"Donna what is this," cried Bat, "What have you done?"

"What have I done? What the hell could I have done you

moron?" I barked. "You've had me held captive in this bathroom."

Bang. The door crashed inward again and my second superhero, Donny, appeared in the doorway.

"What are you all doing in the ladies' room?" he posed quizzically.

Another bang, and the door crashed in yet again. This time my superheroes were Babs and Peg brandishing some serious weaponry.

"Everybody just stay where you are," bellowed Peg.

They had definitely been watching too many cop shows. And speaking of cops – right about then we heard the fourth and nearly final bang. This time when the door crashed open, my entire squad of detectives and uniforms poured in from the hallway.

" Hands up, dirtbag," Warren shouted.

Bang again. Who else? It was Clovis. And the true mystery here was not the murder of Claire, but rather the ability of Clovis to somehow take this cacophony of confusion and turn the whole thing around to be about her. No one could ever deny that woman has talent. I'm not at all sure it's a marketable talent – but talent nonetheless.

Warren's men grabbed Bat and began to handcuff him. My various superheroes were comparing notes as to how and why they'd all arrived in this bathroom – it was a madhouse – a very cramped and noisy madhouse.

"Oh my god," Clovis shrieked. "Why is this all happening to me?"

For a little thing she had some set of lungs. All action stopped and eyes were on Clovis. Slowly she turned to square off and face

Bat eye to eye. And then she said: "Detective Warren, do you think Bat will be going to prison for a very long time?"

That was it. My lights went out. Later on they told me that my knees just buckled – probably from the intense terror of being held hostage by an admitted murderer who had also admitted that he'd planned to kill me – or maybe it was just the colossal weight of Clovis' self-involvement. We'll never really know. Later, when I awoke I was in the parking lot on an ambulance stretcher. They weren't taking any chances. I was hooked up to oxygen and feeling pretty good, and with the oxygen mask on my face there was no pressure to talk – that felt really good.

"Well, Donna you should feel really proud of yourself," beamed Kyle, "You cracked this case."

Unable to answer, I frowned and shook my head. I had absolutely not solved this case. But apparently someone had and that may have saved my life.

[CHAPTER 41]

I was released from my obligatory trip to the hospital within an hour and escorted to the station house by my guard detail, Riley and O'Dowd. They had wanted to summon Jon, but I convinced them not to alarm him as Bat's plans had been thwarted and I was perfectly fine. Besides it was already feeling like a three ring circus! The whole gang was there, each giving statements for use in Bat's trial. Once there, I learned that little Miss Clovis had been arrested as an accessory although they didn't really expect the charges to stick. I think they were just messing with her. Don't they realize being arrested is like a dream come true for a narcissistic wing nut like her?

At the station I learned that Kyle had gotten free from his client meeting and checked his e-mail. The recent e-mail from him to me that he knew he hadn't sent put him instantly on alert. He bolted out the door, frantic to get to the Holiday Inn and terrified of what he would find. He'd barely reached Dodge when his phone rang and it was Donny. Donny's team had determined that Bat was the most likely killer and he wanted to warn both of us to be careful. Kyle filled him in on my imminent danger and Donny made a beeline to the parking garage. His blood was boiling.

In the meantime, Liv's team had come to the same conclusion and Liv was explaining their reasoning to Peg. With her usual antennae in fine working order Peg told Liv that something was going down at that moment. Once Liv heard about Kyle's hasty departure she called his cell and heard enough to convince her to alert Detective Warren.

How Clovis found out about all of this we'll never really know. Some have speculated that she'd had our offices bugged. Who knows?

Speaking of Clovis, apparently they decided that they didn't have enough to hold her on so she was released. When I first heard of this I was extremely concerned for her welfare – how would she cope with not being the center of a highly visible trial – that would be quite a blow. Not to worry, though, she had a plan. She'd already hired O.J.'s attorney and was planning on having Bat fight this bum rap to the death. Yes, there was that minor detail of his full confession – which he repeated to the police and everyone else while crowded in the ladies' room. That would not deter Clovis. Apparently, according to his attorney, I had clearly tricked him into thinking he was the murderer and he was still under my magical spell when the police busted into the crapper.

After the police dropped me off in the Holiday Inn parking lot, I was headed to my car when I heard a familiar voice that struck terror deep into my soul.

"Yoo hoo, Donna," Clovis sang perkily, "Let me tell you my

news!"

I had to be hallucinating, right? This couldn't be happening to me after everything I'd already been through tonight. Maybe if I just ignored it…

"Donna dear, I wanted you to be the first to know since you've been such a dear dear friend to both Bat and me," Clovis gushed.

Oh god, I might as well just face it. Especially since I couldn't really see any means of escaping.

"Hello Clovis," I replied tiredly. "What's on your mind?"

"Well Donna, I wanted you to be the first to know that Bat and I are officially engaged," said Clovis still gushing.

Of course, if you couldn't be a prisoner you could, at least, marry one. It made perfect sense.

"Congratulations Clovis. When's the big day?" I mustered feebly.

"Well, you know I hired that big time attorney to defend Bat, right Donna?" Clovis preened. "So I figure it will be a year or so before it comes to trial and then the trial should take six months to a year. Once we're through all of that and Bat is in prison I figure it will take me another six to eight months to plan a wedding. I'd already done some research on conjugal honeymoons – I figured it was only a matter of time before Bat landed himself in prison for something."

Maybe I'm slow, but let me get this straight. Bat confessed but Clovis insisted on hiring an attorney to get him off, but she doesn't expect to get him off. Maybe it's me but that sounded a little convoluted even for Clovis.

"I know I'm going to be sorry I asked this, Clovis," I began haltingly, "but you expect Bat to get convicted?"

"Well, of course, Donna," she answered a tad peevishly, "I mean, he did kill her after all. And I am very much in favor of justice. Of course I would prefer he not get a death sentence – that would really mess up my wedding plans – I mean we could still have a wedding with him on death row, but he wouldn't really be able to help in the raising of our kids –and I want a family right away. I think having a family while you're still young enough is crucial, don't you agree?"

Now, I had to genuinely ask myself who was the crazy here. Even knowing Clovis as I did I could not imagine that she had actually just said that. I know I heard it, so maybe that makes me the crazy. Either way I just did not have the energy to try and respond to anything this remarkable. I looked around for a means of escape. Maybe if I popped her one she'd lose consciousness just long enough for me to make my getaway. The police cruiser still hovering at the entrance to the parking lot made me think better of that method of escape. Aw hell, I supposed I'd have to talk my way out of this little encounter – and that meant I had to give it some thought. Just as I started to believe that my little gray matter was actually starting to smoke, Clovis took bizarre to yet another level.

"So Donna, I really hope you'll be my matron of honor," Clovis gushed proudly. "I mean, if I ever doubted your love and devotion to me you've certainly proved yourself beyond a shadow of a doubt throughout this whole investigation. Why I can't think of anyone to whom I feel closer."

I was at a fork in the road. The one path would lead me out of crazy, but that path was strewn with life-threatening dangers and it was a very long path. The other path led me right into the heart of the crazy – but it was by far the easier road considering present company. Ah hell, I'm no hero.

"Why Clovis, I'd be honored to serve as your matron of honor. I do hope we'll be wearing very frilly pale pink dresses – that's so me," I responded with an amazingly straight face.

"Oh you know, Donna I hadn't thought it through that far, but I do believe very feminine pink dresses would be the perfect complement to my bridal gown. I think maybe some big floppy hats to go along with the dresses, what do you think?"

Great, if the day ever came when I had to succumb to this gypsy tribal dance, at least I'd get a costume party out of the deal. I could only hope that by the time the wedding was held, I'd have fallen from grace, and in reality I thought that was a pretty safe bet. I was really tired and I wanted to get home. I said my good-byes to Clovis and pointed my car due west.

[CHAPTER 42]

Back home I wasted no time in going to the secret hiding place where Jon's guess at the murderer resided. I grabbed the piece of paper and opened it to see one word written in Jon's familiar penmanship: Bat.

"Damn," I said to the sound of light chuckling.

I turned and Jon was standing in the doorway.

"I take it the murder's been solved?" he asked knowingly.

We spent a couple of hours discussing the evening's events and Jon filled me in on the deductive reasoning that led to his conclusion. I've seen him do it a million times, but he never ceases to amaze me.

After our intense debriefing, Jon and I shared a quick meal of Costco ravioli. That was a bit of a cheat from my usual diet, but I was celebrating still being alive as well as the fact that Claire's murderer was behind bars where he could not hurt me, nor could he bore me into wishing I were dead.

After dinner we settled down to watch a Woody Allen movie, each of us holding a dog on our lap and the third lying between us, taking turns pawing first Jon and then me for attention. Normally on these quiet contemplative evenings we reach for a murder mystery to watch – but for some reason neither one of us seemed to be in the mood.

And speaking of mood. The minute I walked into the office the next morning I sensed a totally altered mood from that of the past week. It felt like a breath of spring. No oppressively heavy fear or distrust. We were safe from the murderer and it wasn't any of us. As I headed down the hall toward my office I could hear the various iterations of numerous aspects of last night's drama being revealed, and as I passed each group I received a hero's welcome and a boatload of questions. It was incredibly heartwarming. They really cared.

I got to my office to find a whole host of e-mails and voicemails all congratulating me on cracking the case and remarking on my courage under fire. All in all, I think most people had a romanticized version of what went down and of my role in the whole extravaganza. In reality I'd felt more like a pawn getting batted around a chess board, but what the hell, if people wanted a hero who was I to deprive them? The calls came in from all over. I even heard from Tina and Cindy, the lady wrestler. Tina wanted me to know that insurance boy was almost definitely headed for prison himself, since they'd been able to find some pretty damning evidence thanks to Claire's murder investigation. The lady wrestler was surprisingly exuberant over my safe recovery. She wanted me to seriously consider wrestling her on a regular basis and she was sure recent news of the solved murder investigation and my involvement would help put butts in the seats. Yep, that was my goal, professional wrestling with a larger than life crowd to witness my full glory. I had to admit there were days when that would sound tempting.

After reviewing and responding to my messages, it was time I made the rounds of the agency to thank all of my unsung heroes. I saw Liv and Donny in the creative living room. They had just come to the disappointing conclusion that both teams had solved the murder at precisely the same time – using two completely different methodologies. I was more than a little relieved about that. Had one triumphed over the other there would be hell to pay, and I would be firmly stuck in the middle. I communicated my sincere appreciation for everything they'd done to keep me safe. When I left them they were arguing over whose methodology was more likely to resolve a broader spectrum of problems needing solutions. I smiled – we would never have a chance to get stagnant.

Moving along the hallway I made it a point to thank each and every one of Donny and Liv's team members. Without their solid contributions I'd hate to think what might have happened in that darkened and deserted ladies' room.

Next it was time to thank Babs and Peg. How could a thank you ever truly convey my appreciation? These woman had been in the trenches with me – at times actually ducking debris from our self-imposed war zones. After all they'd been through, they eagerly risked their necks to save mine yet one more time in that ladies' room. At the rate I was going I would never be able to attend a function at the Holiday Inn and use that ladies' room without misting up, and thanks to menopause I don't need any more opportunities to get misty eyed! I gave my girls a big hug and headed over to Kyle's office.

Just as I was about to launch into my truly heartfelt thank you, his phone rang. I gave him a signal and headed on back to my office. There was a Post-it note. My heart skipped a half a beat while I admonished myself for overreacting to a common office occurrence. The note read: "I need to talk – it's urgent – meet me in front of the building at five." Oh you've GOT to be kidding! Does someone really think this is funny? I am going to find out who did this and kick their ass! Just as I was working myself up into a full blown lather Kyle scurried into my office. The look on his face did not bode well. I waited.

"Donna, it was her," Kyle began obviously quite agitated.

"Her who, Kyle?" I asked skeptically.

"You know, Donna," he parried back at me.

"I really don't, Kyle," I responded more firmly.

"Oh all right, I guess I have to say it," Kyle gulped, "It was Clovis."

Okay, now my heart skipped a full beat.

"Kyle," I whined, "Will we ever escape?"

"No Donna," Kyle replied dejectedly, "We won't."

"I know that I will live to regret asking this question, but what does she want now?" I asked wearily.

"Well Donna, she's pretty upset," Kyle prompted.

"I'll bite, now why?" I countered disgustedly.

"Well Donna, she's facing a huge problem and she would like us to meet her for drinks so that we can help get her through this new crisis," Kyle revealed quickly.

For the life of me I could not imagine what world-shattering crisis could occur to get me to agree to meet Clovis for drinks. Hell could freeze over and my ears could fall off and I would not meet with Clovis if that were the only way I could prevent it. So my answer was simple, No! And that started to make me feel happy. I would just tell her no. That was easy and painless, and that's what would make me happy. I mean it's not like I owed her anything. So nothing that Kyle could say was going to upset me. The answer was no.

But my curiosity got the better of me.

"So what's her problem?" I asked mentally leaning a little too far over to the dark side.

"Well here's the thing, Donna," Kyle replied no less reluctantly. "That hot shot attorney she hired to defend Bat has completed his initial analysis of the case and he's pretty sure he can get the whole thing thrown out of court. Clovis is beside herself. That would mean that she'd lose all those months of working closely with the attorney, all the months of the trial and her big prison wedding and conjugal honeymoon. Donna, I can honestly say I have never heard Clovis this upset."

"You're not actually suggesting that we meet her for drinks to help plot a strategy that will foil the attorney's attempts to free Bat are you?" I asked peering through narrowed eye slits.

"Well, I just can't think of any way to get out of this," Kyle reasoned. "And, I think if we just have one drink..."

"No, Kyle, no I cannot agree to meeting her under any

circumstances!" I declared adamantly. "There's just no way."

Kyle and I politely discussed Clovis' request for another few minutes. Needless to say we met her in front of the building at 5:00 that night. Some things never change!

The End

All characters in this book have no existence outside the imagination of the author, and have no relation whatsoever to anyone bearing the same name or names. Some of the important characters are vaguely inspired by individuals known to the author.

Marcel is a fictional ad agency. None of these people exist and none of these incidents have occurred.

ABOUT THE AUTHOR

Robin Donovan is the author of the blog, Menologues, a humorous yet informative look at the trials and tribulations of menopause by someone who's been there. Menologues is republished on two commercial sites: Vibrant Nation and Alltop, and has won regional honors for social media at the AMA Pinnacles and PRSA Paper Anvil awards.

Donovan was born and raised in New Jersey but lived and worked in Connecticut for a number of years before moving to Nebraska in 1999. Starting her career as a high school English teacher, Donovan moved into advertising in the early 80's. In 1999 she accepted a job offer from Bozell, an Omaha based ad agency. In late 2001, she and three colleagues purchased Bozell from its New York based parent company.

Donovan lives with her husband and three bulldogs, Roxi, Sadie (Sweet Pea) and Frank.

I DIDN'T KILL HER,
BUT THAT MAY HAVE BEEN SHORT SIGHTED

(2nd in the series of Donna Leigh mysteries)

It was Wednesday and I was running a bit late. I ran across the partner parking lot with my pocketbook and tote bag in one hand and my 12-pack of Diet Orange Sunkist in the other. Burdened with an unwieldy and increasingly heavy load I navigated precariously through both the front door and the lobby entrance. Once inside I wound my way around pods and desks balancing awkward parcels as I progressed. Reaching my desk, I quickly dispatched the various and sundry paraphernalia and logged on to my computer. I had a 10 am conference call and I wanted to reread the client's file before jumping on the phone.

I noticed my message light blinking and hoped it would be something quick. No time to fool around if I was going to review that file. The message was from Ken Farley. It was kind of a blast from the past. I had worked with Ken at an ad agency in southern

Connecticut for a number of years, which now seemed like a lifetime ago. Ken's message was oddly cryptic.

He said "Wow, Donna, that must have been some shock for you, huh? Guess you're having trouble deciding whether it's a good shock or a bad one."

Geez was Ken on the sauce now, I wondered. I couldn't imagine what on earth he could be talking about. Oh well, no point in taxing my brain I might as well just call him. I know I should have waited but that damn curiosity got the best of me. Once on the phone Ken was no less cryptic. I put up with about two minutes of his nonstop gibberish before I really started to lose my temper.

"HEY, KEN," I bellowed, "what the hell are you talking about?!"

That seemed to help him focus.

"You mean you haven't heard?" he asked incredulously, once he'd realized I had no idea what he was saying.

"Guess not," I replied trying to hold on to what was left of my patience, "why don't you fill me in?"

"Your old buddy bought the farm, Donna," Ken announced triumphantly, "Betty Jean."

"Thornton?" I barked emphatically.

"That's what I'm saying" Ken pressed, "you didn't hear about it?"

"How would I have heard about it all the way here in Omaha?" I asked with irritation, he really could be thick sometimes.

"Man Donna, you don't know that either?" Ken sounded

272

astonished. "Didn't you know she moved to Omaha three months ago?"

The man was talking pure nonsense now. Betty Jean and I had worked together for several years when I was in the Connecticut marketplace. I had moved to Omaha 10 years before and had seen neither hide nor hair of B.J. for, at least two, years prior to that, which was definitely how I liked it. Betty Jean move to the heartland – never! She fancied herself a big city player and a fashionista. There was no way she was moving to Omaha, Nebraska.

"Ken, I'm sure you're mistaken, Betty Jean would no sooner move to Omaha than I would move to Appalachia…"

"But Donna, that's where you're wrong," Ken corrected me patiently, "she did move to Omaha, and now she's dead."

Now my head was starting to hurt. I heard what he was saying but it just wasn't possible. In the past Ken had always been a good source of information. A career pr guy he took pride in knowing not only what was going on, but why. Maybe it was time to shut up and let Ken fill in the blanks. Shutting up was not my best thing!

"Donna I honestly can't believe you didn't know B.J. was in Omaha," Ken continued, "she'd been telling everyone she was moving there so the two of you could go into business together. In fact there was even an article in the Times Courier just as she was preparing to move."

Ken took a slight break here. Good thing because I was pretty sure I felt something in my head pop. If there was bleeding in the brain I'd want to clear the line and dial 911. My life must have been flashing before my eyes because I started seeing images of the past. I had worked with Betty Jean at my first advertising agency, the one I joined after making the move from teaching English. She was my immediate supervisor. And she hated my guts. So her supervisory skills consisted of emotional abuse and abject criticism. At times I even caught wind of her fabricating work order memos which she addressed to me, but never delivered, so she could complain about my incompetence. She was often heard announcing to anyone within earshot that I'd lost yet another memo. B. J. made sure that her fraudulent documents were hidden far from my sight, and I would never have had proof of her duplicity had it not been for her sloppy work habits. She left evidence of her betrayal lying around in various unfinished stages where my fair minded colleagues could not help but find it and piece together a clear picture of her diabolical master plan. I shuddered as I recalled that disconcerting time in my early career, when I learned that talent and brains are not always enough, and that there were people who would expend energy to deliberately hurt someone else. Although I was to see additional proof of this, occasionally, over the years, I continue to be baffled by the logic behind such cowardly behavior.

Even with conclusive proof in hand, my vindication was subdued at best. When you're as slippery as B. J. it isn't tough to weasel out of even the tightest of jams. It didn't hurt that she was handling all the media for our largest aerospace account, and the boss needed her more than she did me. It was a lesson in office politics which formed that little bit of paranoid edge that would serve me well as I climbed the advertising ladder. We damn sure never learned about the mean streets teaching high school.

Remarkably, I let this torture continue for about three and a half years. To the uninitiated I would appear to be an idiot not to have gotten the hell out of there ASAP. But in the dog eat dog world of agency business, I was industriously building my resume and my skill set by learning as much as humanly possible at one of the two most acclaimed ad agencies in Connecticut. I was loathe to jeopardize this rare opportunity; to do so would have been career suicide. At any rate, over time even B.J. had to acknowledge that I was a reliable and talented employee. A fact which only served to make it easy for her to dump all her work on me, so she did.

No, going into business with Betty Jean was never a consideration for me, although she did approach me, indirectly, about starting a business when I was working in the New Haven market. My answer back then was an uncategorical "no", and now was no different. Besides, I already had two business partners with whom I owned the Omaha-based ad agency, Marcel. Even if B.J. and I didn't have a history of hostility I would be hard pressed to convince my partners to allow her to waltz in as a fourth owner.

"Ken, you're sure this isn't some lame practical joke?" I asked as I made my way, headphone firmly in place, to the nearest conference room and firmly latched the door. Sure, it might be too late but I didn't really want this news blasted out to the entire staff, at least not yet.

Several months earlier, Marcel had moved its Corporate headquarters from comfortable, new construction suburbia into a classic, historic, downtown loft, replete with high ceilings, exposed brick and pipes along with a few unwelcome surprises that would emerge along the way. Our new setting was the perfect place to ditch the old fashioned, isolated executive offices and opt for a far more collaborative and integrated environment. It created a surprisingly energized atmosphere, making us wonder why we hadn't made the change earlier. Naturally, there are inherent challenges in any work environment. Having to be cognizant of the content and volume of phone calls was one of those challenges, but the head phones and additional conference space made it unquestionably doable.

"I'm dead serious, Donna, oh geez, that was tacky," Ken blathered nervously.

So typically Ken, even in a crisis he couldn't stop with the lame jokes.

"Wow, it's hard to believe B.J. is really dead," I hesitated. "Where did she die?"

"In the office space she had leased to go into business with you from what I heard. But Donna," Ken continued tentatively, "They're saying she was murdered."

Now I was pretty sure I was home in bed having a bizarre dream. Too many ridiculous notions all at one time. This just couldn't be real. I started to think about what I'd eaten before going to bed. It must really have disagreed with my whole digestive system to give me such crazy assed dreams. I started to wonder if I could will myself awake when my reverie was disturbed by Ken's voice.

"Hey Donna you still there?" he whispered sheepishly.

"Wouldn't have expected to be dreaming about Betty Jean and Ken." I mused.

"You're not dreaming, Donna. It's all real." Ken assured me.

"Can't be." I countered. "I've gone all these years never knowing anyone who was murdered. And now, within just a few months of each other, two of the women who have labored to make my working life a living hell have been murdered right here, practically in my back yard. "

"What Donna? Do you need to go online and check one of your local news sites? Go ahead, I'll wait." Ken prompted.

I didn't know what I hoped to accomplish but I ran back to my desk and popped the url of one of our local news sites into my computer and began to read about a recently murdered transplant from Connecticut. I was pretty sure that browsers didn't function correctly in dreams – so I had to start believing that this might all be real. It was a lot to swallow at one time. If what Ken was saying was true, I had once again unwittingly become a major player in a murder investigation – and it wasn't even time for lunch yet. My head was really starting to hurt now. If I was having trouble convincing my old pal Ken that I didn't know what B.J. had been doing, how was I going to convince Warren?

Detective Warren was in charge of murder investigations in Omaha. I knew her from a recent murder investigation in which I'd played a fairly major role. The vic, that's how we say victim in law enforcement, had been a former co-worker, Claire Dockens, and the rocky history that she and I had had involved me, in spades. In order to clear myself, my colleague Kyle (another Dockens dissenter) and I had gone about trying to help solve the crime. Although, in retrospect, I have a sense that my involvement only added to the chaos, most folks insist I had singlehandedly solved the mystery. Ken's news alerted me that, mere months after life had settled down on the Dockens murder, we were faced with another murder for which I would have to be the prime suspect. I wasn't sure I was up to that conference call after all.

Just as I was finishing up on my call with Ken, Kyle sauntered into my office with his usual cheerful and upbeat demeanor. I lost no time in filling him in on the whole Thornton problem.

"That's unbelievable, Donna," Kyle squawked clearly in shock, "how could something like this happen again so soon? " And as an afterthought, "Don't worry, Donna, we'll figure this one out together, just like last time!"

God bless Kyle. Kyle Thoroughgood was my crime solving partner as well as my colleague and friend. I knew I could count on him for anything. Last time he and I had both expected to be suspects since we'd both had rocky relationships with the vic. Surprisingly, we didn't get much heat from the cops. Try to keep up with my extensive use of homicide lingo so you don't fall behind.

This time Kyle was willing to jump right in with both feet, even though he'd never heard of the vic until right at that moment. If I remember correctly from our last adventure this would be an incredibly time consuming little hobby, and it had been grueling on Kyle to actively participate in the investigation without falling behind on his extremely demanding work schedule.

Kyle and I were colleagues at Marcel, the only Omaha ad agency with a widely recognized brand. I also happened to own a third of the company the other two thirds were owned by my partners Liv Danielson and Donny Miller.

"You know, Donna, now that I think of it I do remember hearing about that murder on the news. And it sounded very odd. Maybe you should call Warren before she has a chance to come after you," Kyle suggested thoughtfully.

Probably good advice. But not something I'd look forward to doing.

Made in United States
North Haven, CT
28 May 2022

19580874R10168

Matthew Arnold